Joseph McGee Private Investigator: Book Five

THE BOSS'S DAUGHTERS

McGee Works for a Mob Boss

Carl Douglass

Neurosurgeon Turned Author Writes With Gripping Realism

Since 1978

PO Box 221974 Anchorage, Alaska 99522-1974
books@publicationconsultants.com—www.publicationconsultants.com

ISBN 978-1-59433-592-1
eISBN 978-1-59433-593-8
Library of Congress Catalog Card Number: 2015955403

Manufactured in the United States of America.

Dedication

To those who work to save children.

Chapter One

C innamon Paxton, age eleven, and Paprika, age nine— her sister—are as nearly inseparable as sisters can be. Although they are in different grades at school—Harlem World Academy Lower School—they see each other at recess, lunch, assemblies, and all school activities. The two girls attend the same church—Universal Church—are in the same Girl Scout troop, play computer games together, and are part of the same small circle of BFFs with few friends or acquaintances outside that circle. By the sheerest of coincidences, they share the same birthday, two years apart. The sisters live with their mother in a very expensive five-story condominium on 142 West 129th Street under assumed names. The girls and their mother live separate from their father. That separation came about because the separation of the worlds of their mother and their father is—by mutual choice—necessary to protect the mother and children. The rich, privileged, and carefully protected, girls live in fear. That fear is mainly of their father and the people who surround him in his world.

Very highly trained and capable men and women are on duty to provide security for the children and their mother twenty-four hours a day, seven days a week, 365 days a year, and have been in place since the children were born. The separation of the parents was occasioned when the girls were ages three and five by two acts of serious violence that took place near their former home in South Harlem. Angelina Paxton—the wife and mother—was completely ignorant and naïve about her new husband, Damien Markee, prior to their marriage. When the scales fell from her eyes and she came to realize what Damien's livelihood and life entails, she grew up rapidly and issued an ultimatum—either he renounce his involvement with the BK [Black Knights] for a respectable life with her and their children; or the two spouses will have to live apart. Divorce is out of the question—they are Catholics, he is a controlling and an alpha male; and besides, as king of the BK, Damien is disinclined to abandon the enormously lucrative ongoing criminal enterprise he controls. For that matter, walking away from the gang is quite literally impossible to do and to survive. Damien and Angelina—real name, Deshawn—agree to live separately despite all of the security issues and inconveniences that entails.

She does not want to assume a new identity and to live apart from her husband, but he convinces her that it is altogether necessary. An accumulation of events after the separation further convinces Angelina of the wisdom of maintaining separate and secret lives, and she accepts the profound change in her life with conviction that it is the only acceptable alternative. Violence involving her husband makes the news with unnerving frequency, and—try as she might—Angelina is not able to shield her children from knowing about their father and what he does for a living. It is probably for the best that they receive frequent reminders because it keeps them wary and convinced that they must never make a mistake and reveal who their father is and what he does.

After six years in the beautiful new school for Cinnamon and four years for Paprika, the student body and faculty have become accustomed to the presence of the bodyguard contingent. Security personnel are not at all uncommon in the exclusive and prestigious K-12 school. Cinnamon and Paprika—like their classmates—make a determined effort not to pay attention to the security men and women and their guns. On any given day, about a dozen men and women sit watching their young charges or take turns patrolling the hall. The important children of important people never quibble about the presence of so many armed officers. The general consensus is that it would be unforgivable to have their child go to school and be killed there by a loony. Nobody has any 'icky-poo' liberal nonsense about guns, metal detectors, x-ray machines when required, or pat-downs. They want their children to come home safe every day.

This particular day is Cinnamon and Paprika's birthday, and for lunch there is a birthday party for the entire school paid for by the girls' father, Damien Markee. Only the head of the lower school—as it is commonly called—knows that Damien is the children's father, and for this—as for many other occasions—he is an anonymous donor. Cinnamon is sitting with Paprika and two special friends who help them open cards from every faculty member, administrator, janitor, security officer, and student. No gifts are allowed to make it possible to honor every child on his or her birthday without going broke buying presents or crazy trying to keep up with anything more than a card made from colored card stock with a very short personal note.

Pizza, chocolate cupcakes, and milk are the food groups chosen for the occasion as they are for almost every birthday at the school. Cinnamon especially loves parties, and she and Paprika have a great time laughing at the funny notes written by their favorite people. They have to wait an extra hour after school because their security unit is a man short, and they are reluctant to join the large crowd leaving the school grounds immediately after the last bell rings. Hank Duffy—former MMA fighter and Navy SEAL—developed a bleeding ulcer just before Cinnamon and Paprika were to be picked up for their ride to school that morning, and a certified substitute is not available on such short notice for the escorted ride home.

Chapter Two

Damien Markee holds court in two locations in New York City. This is his day to deal with the nitty-gritty in his East Harlem Men's Club on 133rd Street two doors away from a derelict plant on Riverside Drive in Spanish Harlem. The men's club is a long-term holdover from the days when East Harlem was accurately known as "Black Mecca." Harlem's black population peaked in the 1950s. In 2008, the Census found that for the first time Harlem's population was no longer a majority black, with their share now reduced to 40 percent and is more accurately called "Spanish Harlem."

In the late 1940s, African-American veterans began returning from World War II expecting to find a changed America more in conformance with the partial acceptance of equality they had experienced in the military. They were sadly mistaken and understandably angry when they found the Jim Crow laws still in full flower, and the opportunities for gainful employment more often than not closed to them on the basis of their skin color. Some veterans accepted the status quo and a bitter assimilation into the "Whites Only" society. Many joined the exodus—the "Second Great Migration" from the rural South with all of its cruel discrimination and found their places in the teeming inner-city ghettoes. The motto of Harlem became "Making It," and the draw to the neighborhood was overwhelming. Living there was better than in the South, but most of the people of color eked out a meager living doing the menial tasks that required minimal education that Whites were loath to do. A few combat-hardened men elected to follow suit with their Jewish counterparts in the Kosher Nostra and their Italian competitors in La Cosa Nostra building formidable criminal empires.

In that era, Harlem—especially East Harlem—was their territory, and the Black Knights established their foothold. Jackson "Killer Knight" Jones was the first black man to achieve godfather status—to use the Mafia terminology—and he established a highly successful criminal syndicate that dominated Harlem. Although he ran a stern protection racket in the African-American community, he actually gave the citizens good protection and was wise enough to recognize that if his neighborhood flourished, so would he and his gang. Jones left the army as a first lieutenant, one of a handful of colored men to achieve officer rank. He was a genius in the controlling, rewarding, and disciplining men, and a very capable administrator who recognized his limitations. Taking a lesson from the mafia organizations that bore sway over the rest of the five boroughs, Jones hired able attorneys, accountants, and recruiters. He quickly acquired the finest police officers, judges, prosecutors, aldermen, state house representatives, and even two congressmen and a senator that money could buy. He was selective in gathering about him fanatically loyal and capable soldiers and security personnel, and paid them well and promoted them with fairness and evenness.

Jackson Jones and his loyalists lived in a state of almost constant war—a condition for which five years of army combat had amply prepared them. They fought to preserve their territory, their people, and their criminal livelihoods from the incursions of the Italian, Polish, and Jewish criminal elements that—more often than not—required the shedding of blood and the loss of life. In so doing they materially contributed to the officially earned title for Harlem of "The Murder Capital of America." Police statistics from 1940 on showed about 100 murders per year in Harlem. By 1950, essentially all of the whites had left Harlem. Police service in the two NYPD precincts serving East Harlem—the 23rd and 25th— was considered hazardous duty and a combat zone with areas that cops would not enter without a tank. For the industrious officer who was unhampered by a conscience, East Harlem was a great place to become quietly rich.

The old saw that "Those who live by the sword will die by the sword" was altogether a truism in the neighborhood and among the Black Knights. "Killer Knight" Jones recognized that his was a profession that did not promise longevity. There were old Black Knights, bold Black Knights, but precious few old and bold Black Knights. Once he had the money, Jones made a residential move that emulated the rest of New Yorkers who were becoming affluent. He "moved up" to a beautiful brownstone on West 143rd Street between Amsterdam Avenue and Convent Avenue, in Hamilton Heights—the Hamilton Grange neighborhood.

The neighborhood was part of what was known as "Sugar Hill." Sugar Hill got its name because residents from areas of central Harlem and parts of the rest of the five boroughs aspired to move "up the hill" to the part of town where handsome brownstones, spacious and airy apartments, and buildings of sound architectural structure and enviable design abounded, and amenities enjoyed by the nouveau riche all around the United States were demanding were to be found if you had the cash. "Moving up the hill" was an undeniable prestige factor. It meant that you were rich, no matter what your color or religion was; you had made it to the land where living was sweet as sugar.

Jackson "Killer Knight" Jones ensconced his family in Sugar Hill and established a double life of uptown legitimacy for his family while he pursued his real livelihood down in "the Mecca." Jones was murdered by a mafia hit man in 1956. The Black Knights retaliated in such an overkill orgy of revenge that the Italians never again attempted a takeover or a threat to the territory ruled by the BK. Eleven "generals" of the BK—as they became known over the years—died violent deaths between 1956 and 2006 when Damien Markee rose meteorically from the ranks to assume the generalship. He was the first BK leader to have a college degree; in fact, he graduated from Columbia Business School with a BS in business management and the CUNY School of Law with honors. That alone—however useful—would not have brought him to the attention of the BK leaders. But his incomparable skills in the martial arts and use of most other equipment of death, total disregard for the lives of his enemies and competitors, and his brilliance in attaining and maintaining a clean police record while killing off his would-be opponents for the top position, earned him full respect—a status based on a bone-marrow level of fear by his allies and enemies alike.

He even took over—by a peaceful purchase—the splendid brownstone in Hamilton Heights originally owned by the Jackson Jones estate. There—like any self-respecting Mafia don—Damien Markee entertained police commissioners, entertainers, politicians, churchmen, self-appointed black spokesmen, doctors, lawyers, and the glitterati of all stripes. There he lived the sweet "Sugar Hill" life, and—like the original owner of the mansion—also conducted his other life in the poverty-stricken ghetto of East Harlem just above the invisible but easily identifiable line between "the upper east side" and the ravages of Harlem above 98th Street.

Among the guests in the Hamilton Heights mansion are Friday night poker game regulars—friends with no illusions about who Damien Markee is or how he makes his fortune. Those friends include the sitting mayor of New York, Franklin Delancy; Charles Daniels, the billionaire husband of the DCIA [Director of the Central Intelligence Agency]; Ivory White, a former senior officer in the BK, now a partner with P.A.M.J. McGee and Caitlin O'Brian—formerly an NYPD detective—in McGee & Associates Investigations; Gen. Mark Dantelle, USA Ret., a former associate of Damien during his brief military service; and Dominic Lanza, current don of the original Colombo Sicilian crime syndicate. By mutual agreement this group of friends accepts that business, politics, religion, and race are taboo subjects. It is absolutely forbidden for any business activity or connection to be entered into between any of the members of the Friday poker night group.

This is Tuesday afternoon, so business is being conducted in the unofficial headquarters of the BK—the East Harlem Men's Club on 133rd Street. Damien Markee asked for the meeting, and it is a sign of cautious mutual trust that all invitees are present. Damien—like all crime lords—has a nickname, "The Kiss," a reference to a certain facial expression Damien has when he is delivering the kiss of death. The nickname is never used in Damien's presence. Besides "The Kiss,"

Don Dominic Lanza from the Colombo family; Leopoldo Rodriguez, the head of the New Conquistadores—the Puerto Rican syndicate that now controls Spanish Harlem; Bart Derekson from the Hells Angels; and, incongruously, Most Rev. Dany J. Khallouf, bishop of the Eparchy of Brooklyn Maronites—present as a buffer among the less savory attendees—are the other men seated in the back room of the Men's Club.

All of the men have a lunch imported from Spain of calçots grilling onions, tapas, cured Serrano and Ibérico hams, paella, and Don Rodriguez's favorite sangria—a chilled combination of Rioja red wine, brandy, brown sugar, and ginger ale with the juice of fresh lemon and orange wedges. It is time for business.

"Thank you, gentlemen," Damien says. "We are all busy men; so, I will keep this short and simple."

"Simple so us peasants can understand, Damien?" Don Dominic asks with a smile.

"Not for everyone—just for the Sicilians, Dominic."

They all laugh, and any remaining tension subsides. If they can share gentle ethnic jokes without rancor, they should be able to consider a mutually beneficial business arrangement.

"Let me assure you that the place has been scrubbed clean of bugs. The police don't come here unless they are invited—which is rare—and we have never had a listening device placed in the men's club. To be safe, my security people swept it just an hour ago. We can speak frankly.

"I have been thinking lately how well we are getting along, as different as we are in background and approach. Police statistics show there were only nine murders in Spanish Harlem last year, and that is a trend that is holding. Rapes and burglaries are also way down. I am of the opinion that our restraint in dealing with each other is the main reason for that drop in crime where we live. I—for one—want things to stay that way. It is good for business. There was a time in the city when the heads of the five Sicilian families met and formed a council where they made rules and decided and enforced discipline. They made acceptable zones of interest and left each other alone for a time and prospered.

"Times have changed. Back then, the dons had real control and received respect. Back then, this was Italian Harlem and the Cosa Nostra under the Genovese Family ruled, then it was Black Harlem and the Black Knights ruled. Now, in the twenty-first century, it is Spanish Harlem, and the Latin Kings rule under Don Leopoldo. That is the reality. There are lots of Puerto Ricans—almost 60 percent. Maybe something less than 40 percent African-Americans, and compared to the heyday of the Cosa Nostra here, only a few Italians left. There is a great deal of money to be made here. The rackets are still doing pretty well, but the state lottery has cut in on us in a big way. We still have the girls, the abandoned warehouse fights, and the union, city, and state contributions. The Italians have not made it a matter of war to lose their once complete control of the cops, the politicians, the unions, and the building trades and the trash collection cuts. In return, we have given up a share of the girls, the rackets, and the state money.

"We need to form a council to make sure everybody is happy, rich, and safe. So, I am going to make you an offer. Without expecting anything in return except cooperation, I will help you get a hand into our enterprises in LA, Phoenix, Chicago, Philly, New Jersey, and Miami. Our suppliers for nose candy and some of the other pharmaceuticals is problematic, but our distribution system is great. Maybe we can work something out there. Maybe we can share our contacts with law enforcement and the courts. We all are doing pretty well in that regard; so, by sharing, we might make our businesses more secure and lucrative."

"Who'd be the big boss of this new arrangement, Damien?" Don Leopoldo asks.

"Why, me, of course, and you can all serve me in a happy plantation sort of arrangement!" Damien says with a genuine full-face smile and a hearty belly laugh.

"I know you're kidding, Damien, but it'll be a problem. In fact it'll kill the deal if we don't come up with a good solution from the get-go."

"I have an idea."

"Let's hear it."

"All members of the council will be of equal rank from the start. Among ourselves, we will elect an administrator who will be paid a salary for the work of running the organization—say a million a year. There will be a mandatory rotation of the *capo di tutti capi*. I'm not sure how long we want each guy to serve—maybe three years; so, he can get into a good grove—but no possibility of reelection until everyone of us has had a turn. We will need to make up a constitution; so, we don't get a dictatorship going or some kind of "president-for-life" deal. We'll need limitations and responsibilities and a means of peaceful removal of our *capo di tutti capi* if he can't perform or oversteps. What do you think?"

Don Dominic speaks for them all, "We need to sleep on it. Let's meet uptown at my place in a week after we've had time to run the whole idea past our guys and after we have each had a chance to come up with suggestions about this 'constitution' you talked about, Damien."

"Okay, sounds good," Damien says. "Now, I've gotta get home to get ready for my daughter's birthday party."

Chapter Three

Damien takes a cab from the East Harlem Men's Club on 133rd Street to Angelina Paxton's five-story condominium at 142 West 129th Street in uptown Harlem. He directs the cabbie to let him out two blocks away from his wife and children's condo and takes a serious calculated risk to leave his security detail back at the club to avoid calling attention to himself and thereby to the place where his family lives in relative safety under assumed identities. It is only with effort that he avoids demonstrating his usual and obvious self-protective wariness for the same reason.

The brownstone condominium building is very similar to the rest of the buildings in the neighborhood—the 10027 zip code in New York City. Desireé—he refuses to think of her as "Angelina Paxton," a phony identity. The 3,500 square foot, five-story, ten-room, three-bath building was originally constructed in 1893 and reconstructed in 2002. It was recently appraised at $1,921,586, and its value has been increasing every year. The two-family brownstone building includes an owner's triplex and a simplex floor-through rental unit that provides Desireé, Cinnamon, and Paprika a comfortable independent income. Damien has no legal ownership; the condo is owned on paper by the fake person, Angelina Paxton. Damien does not begrudge Desireé the ownership or the profit; she deserves it. Unlike many of the wives and girlfriends of his associates in his business, Desireé has never been a high-maintenance girl, and her demands on him are minimal except for her altogether understandable desire for safety for their daughters. Despite all of his and her precautions, Damien carries a low-grade anxiety that their identities and address may become known, and they may become endangered.

He knocks—although he does not have to—and Desireé admits him into the owner's triplex. As soon as the door closes behind him, Desireé plants a fervent open-mouth kiss and a full body embrace that creates the old stir her body always does. Despite the separate arrangements of their lives, that aspect remains undimmed in its intensity. There is a hurried and chaotic disrobing and a trail of clothing from the entryway to the master bedroom that does not require an Eagle Scout to follow. When the personal heat diminishes, the still loving couple lies close beside each other and begins to talk in the comfort of the condo's central air conditioning and an overhead fan that make this small oasis in the teeming and unseasonably hot city a place of refuge for both of them.

"How's business, Damien?" Desireé asks, as interested as ever in the legitimate side of Damien's interests.

"I'll give us ten years to get completely legit. I have been putting a lot of money into REITs and an investment called the Vulture Fund that buys up properties that have been foreclosed on, fixes them up, and sells them at a profit. I have actually bought two of them, and they bring in about

$12,000 a month after taxes. I should have the principal paid off in ten years."

"Sorry, Damien, you told me before what a REIT is, but I forget."

"Real Estate Investment Trust. You and I own a tree farm, a peach orchard in Georgia; and you own—all by yourself—a huge potato farm someplace in Idaho. Those investments come to completion in five years. We can sell them and move over to some Utah drilling companies which pay a big dividend as they bring up natural gas. America leads the world in natural gas production, and this investment looks like a long-term keeper."

"Well, I'm glad about the Idaho investment. I have always liked huge potatoes," Desireé jokes. "Are you keeping safe with the rest of the business?"

"As a matter of fact, just this morning I set in motion a plan to get my competitors to take a civilized and cooperative deal which should make our lives a lot safer. We'll join instead of continuing to fight. That should ease my way into retirement. I'm hoping that this arrangement will give stability for doing business and help to eliminate problems of succession when my time comes. In the past, most of my predecessors could not find a safe permanent way to leave that end of the business. I'm hoping this idea will make it both safe, easy, and profitable which should make the idea of hostile takeovers less appealing."

Desireé laughs inwardly at Damien's euphemistic description of his business. It is as if he were explaining his most recent spreadsheet for a paper products factory. She smiles.

Among other things Damien loves about his young wife is her easy and toothy smile. She is a beautiful woman with an unblemished café au lait complexion. She has honored his request that she not mark her skin with tattoos or piercings except for earrings, and he is grateful at her willingness given the exploding trend of inking as much skin as possible by both men and women—"tramp stamps" he calls them. Tattoos on women remind him far too much of the drug besotted women he employs in his most lucrative "other business," the one he makes a strong effort never to mention to his wife. Desireé has lustrous thick black hair that has been artfully straightened to hang gently down to the bottom of her neck. Without him asking, she has avoided coloring her hair with some blue or green or purple stripes—also a fashion statement which his drifted snow girls have taken up with enthusiasm. She is small—size 2—and lissome. Her finely chiseled face bespeaks a beauty derived from a fortunate genetic selection.

"Let's talk about the party, Damien. I'm so sorry that you can't be there. The girls understand ... sort of. I want us to be together for a while before the party, probably as soon as they get home from school. What do you think about us having a little late lunch—something simple—at the hotel before everybody starts coming?"

"How can we pull that off? It won't take any feat of genius to become suspicious if they see us together."

"You're not the only one who knows a guy or two who can get things done. I made an executive decision and booked a room at the Carlyle on 76th Street and Madison Avenue under a phony name. You are Lester Givens, and I am your dutiful wife, Katrina. We have a suite, and we can order room service."

Damien laughs. He loves the fine old hotel, which debuted in 1930. He knows that a suite would set him back about $600, and he does not care.

"Get a room with a view?"

"Of course. It's on Madison Avenue overlooking Central Park. And it's luxurious."

"I'll just bet," Damien says. "And, it's known for being a serious purveyor of privacy. Okay, Katrina. Text me the particulars about the room and the time, and I'll be there bearing gifts. You are a prize, and I promise you that your day will come. We'll be legit; and we'll live someplace safe, tropical, and obscure reasonably soon."

Desireé gives him a broad and guiless smile. For him it is reward enough.

"Okay, c'mon girls, it's time to get you home and into your party dresses, then we'll be off to the Carlyle Hotel for a big shebang!" Lydia Fairchild tells them.

Lydia is the senior security officer from the New York Protection Service. She is a former Secret Service agent whose specialty is guarding children. She managed security operations for the previous president's three school-age children. It was her decision to wait until the school clears; so, they will have clear traffic back to the condominium on 142 West 129th Street. She works at not being distracted by the prospects of what her date—her first in almost a year—will be like. He seems like a great guy. Her choice of departure is likely to make them slightly late, but the diminished traffic and a few broken speed limits should let them get to the condo in plenty of time for the girls to get ready.

Lydia and the girls start for the limo. Chet Nichols is outside checking for threats. He motions to Andy Lusesky—the new guy—and Lydia that it is safe to leave the building. The Harlem World Academy Lower School stands on a large campus at 120 West 120th Street three blocks from

Morningside Park, half a block from 7th Avenue, between 7th Ave. (on the east) and Central Park West, which shortly becomes Frederick Douglass Boulevard. The school campus and its buildings are a security guard's nightmare—all open and airy—and with no place to be obscure, let alone to hide. Every day the guards have the same routine that entails serious surveillance and full attention all the time.

Andy comes to the unit as the defensive driving specialist with impressive credentials. He chauffeured foreign diplomats for the Bureau of Diplomatic Security, US Department of State for ten years and remains a defensive driving instructor for the DOD and state. He was wooed away from his regular government career to take a more adventuresome job with the Lanza Family higher-ups. Damien approved him as a substitute for Hank Duffy—who chose this particular day to develop a bleeding ulcer—largely because of his association with the Genovese family bosses. The final choice was Damien's, although Desireé's contacts at the school recommended him first.

The girls know the drill. As soon as Chet opens the door, they run to the backseat of the armored Mercedes S550 Rolls Royce Edition limo, get in as quickly as possible, and lean forward; so, they cannot be seen from outside the vehicle. The limo is as attack-proof as the US vice-president's. Andy guns the powerful engine; and they roll out of the campus and onto the city streets, pushing other cars into other lanes. They make good time until they approach the intersection of Adam Clayton Powell Jr. Boulevard and 125th Street, where there is some sort of police blockade. A uniformed NYPD officer approaches the driver's window and gestures for Andy to open it.

"Sorry for the delay, sir," the officer says. "Accident. We should be cleared in less than five minutes."

It is a commentary on New Yorkers that nobody even pauses to take notice of the accident and the three police vehicles surrounding it, or the sleek black limousine. Andy breaks policy rules and opens the door to step out and look.

Chet says to Lydia, "Hey, the newbie is outside the car; and he left the doors unlocked."

Lydia is about to shrug the minor infraction off; but the start of her comment is interrupted by all six doors of the limo opening at once; and six men in military black outfits and wearing ski masks point Uzis at everyone in the car.

Lydia reaches for her gun and receives a sharp slap across the face.

"No guns. Hands in plain sight. Everybody out! Now!"

Cinnamon and Paprika start to cry. Lydia calms them. Andy, Chet, and Lydia are pulled out onto the street, handcuffed with their hands behind them, hooded, and thrown into the back of a large unmarked van. The two little girls are removed bodily and placed in hoods and wrist and ankle bindings as well. A nondescript four-door Chevy pulls alongside the van, and the girls are lifted into the backseat. As soon as the van and the car drive away—no more than ten seconds after the limousine pulled to a stop—the three cop cars drive off as well, as if they were so blind that they missed the kidnapping. According to the handful of witnesses who were later questioned, someone drove the limo away. The entire scenario was like something out of a movie or TV action show, and had an air of complete unreality. The witnesses were unclear as to whether or not a kidnapping had occurred since the van blocked the view of people on the sidewalk. No one got a license number. No police vehicles were indicated on the precinct logs as having been dispatched to the area, and there was no report of an accident or any other kind of an incident. A *New York Times* reporter covering the police beat is given a brief description of the possible incident and reports it to the editor's desk. It appears at the bottom of page nine, section D, the next day.

Chapter Four

Damien and Desireé sit in their suite in the Carlyle waiting for the security team to call. The girls and their guards should be cleaned up at Desireé's condo by now. Desireé opens her iPhone address book and taps Lydia's number. There is no answer—which is extremely odd—and quite unlike the overly conscientious Lydia to fail to pick up after six rings. She usually responds in one or two.

"Try Chet Nichols," Damien suggests, not as concerned as his wife, "maybe Lydia forgot to charge her cell or turned it off for some reason."

Desireé finds Chet's number and calls. Six rings. Nothing.

Damien's interest is now piqued.

"Do we have a number for the new guy ... what's his name?"

"Andy ... Andy Lusky or something like that."

"Lusesky," Damien remembers.

"I don't have his number."

Damien looks on his cell phone address list then punches the listing for New York Protection Service.

As soon as the call is answered, Damien says, "This is Damien Markee. Put me through to Carl Baird."

"I'm sorry, sir, Mr. Baird is in a meeting. I will leave him a message, and he will call back first thing."

"Get him now. My daughters and their security team are out of contact. Mr. Baird will talk to me immediately."

His voice is calm and quiet, but the menace in his tone carries through the phone as if he had been broadcasting in Yankee stadium to an overflow crowd.

"I'll do my best, sir."

"No. Just do it."

Two minutes later, the CEO is on the line.

"What seems to be the problem, Mr. Markee?"

"My children are out of contact—maybe missing. Tell me what you know from their security team."

"Yes, sir. Hang on while I check."

A minute later, Baird returns, "I can't reach them. They last checked in about an hour ago just as the limo left Harlem World Academy Lower School. No news since. I have three teams on their way to retrace the limo's path. We'll find them. Stay close to your cell."

"I am going to send my people out as well. Don't get into a snit if they cross your path. We are going to know what is going on; and we are going to know that as fast as is humanly possible, Baird. Understood?"

"Clearly. I'll get back to you."

Usually Damien Markee's face is a bland mask when dealing with perceived crises. Now, it is a specter of determination and mounting anger. His jaw muscles are clenched,; his brow is wrinkled; and his mouth is set in a tight-lipped line. It is a face that has made many men cower and beg. Damien is a big man in top physical condition. He is six feet four inches tall and weighs a lean 245 pounds. His muscles are all well-defined—both from his almost religious workout schedule and his thrice weekly martial arts training. Unlike his wife's café au lait skin coloration, Damien's is a very dark brown—almost black. He is dressed in a handmade navy blue custom tailored Saint Laurie Merchant Tailors suit. The suit is an Ivy League cut that hugs his muscular frame. He is wearing a freshly laundered and heavily starched custom French-cuff shirt and 22-carat gold cufflinks. His thousand dollar Gucci Diamante boots were handmade in Casellina, outside of Florence. This is his class-A uniform, the one that his business associates see him in. God save the man who gets to see him in his work clothes—all black SWAT style combat apparel made for physical activity. Sometimes—when absolutely necessary—Damien dons a heavy black retro slaughterhouse bib apron. Grown men all cry when he does. If something has happened to his daughters, he will readily put on his work clothes to deal with the issue.

He punches in his right-hand man—Clarence "The Turk" Appleton's—number and has a terse conversation. He explains the recent events and his concerns.

"Full court press," he says to end the conversation.

"Should we call the police, Damien?" Desireé asks pleadingly, fighting to hold back tears.

"Not yet, Desireé. If they have been taken, we don't want to spook the kidnappers."

Desireé begins to cry softly. She knows her husband all too well; and she knows intellectually, if not emotionally, that he is right.

"What do we do then?"

"We have teams out which will scour Harlem. It is probably nothing, and we'll find them getting an ice-cream cone or something. But—whatever is going on—we will get farther faster if we avoid a police and media circus."

"I'm sure you know best, Damien. But, get them all to hurry. I'm scared."

He is head and shoulders taller than his model-framed wife and outweighs her by 135 pounds. He envelopes her slender body with his huge arms and pulls her tightly against him.

"We'll find them, Babe. You have my word on that."

Fifteen minutes later, Desireé's iPhone sounds its *Love Never Felt So Good* ringtones from the Xscape album. There is no caller ID. She answers on the first ring.

"Angelina Paxton."

An electronically altered voice that sounds something like a C movie Sam Spade, says, "Shut up and listen. We have your daughters. Don't bother trying to find them. They are out of your reach and are safe for now."

"Who is this?" shrieks Desireé.

Damien takes her phone and pushes the speakerphone button.

"Never mind. Just listen. Here's the deal: first, we only talk to you, Mrs. Paxton. We know who your husband is, and we won't deal with him or his people. Second, no cops. We get a hint of cops, and you never see or hear from your brats again. Third, this is a business deal, pure and simple. You pay, and you get them back. You don't pay or if you call in the cops or let your husband's men get involved, you don't. Simple. What you pay is twenty-five mil one week from now. We'll be in touch."

Desireé says, "Are they all right? Where are they? Have you hurt them?" but the line was dead.

She turns her stricken face to her husband's and finds it deadly calm. It is a face she has not seen before, and it is frightening.

"Damien, please don't do anything. We can get the ransom. Our little girls are worth every cent. We can't sacrifice them just for a little money!"

Damien chooses his response carefully, "Look, Desireé, we'll make sure the money is available, but we have no good idea what form the kidnappers want the payment in. What I've heard is that paying the ransom is more likely to get rich children killed than not doing so. As long as they don't have the money, the girls are valuable. Understand?"

"I think so. Actually, I've heard the same thing at a seminar for wealthy women in the city a while ago. I feel so helpless and frustrated. We have to do something."

"While you were on the phone, I got an idea. No matter how hard we try to keep police involvement a secret, the kidnappers are bound to discover what we are doing; so, I think we should comply with the demand to keep them out for now. You remember McGee—the guy I play poker with on Fridays?"

"I think so. He's the private-eye, isn't he?"

"That's him. So far as I know, he is the best of the best. His partner is Ivory White who used to work with me in the BK back in 2006 when I took over from Alphonse Martin. They deal with high-profile issues; they are very effective; and they are extremely discreet. Ivory and McGee can help if anybody can."

"Then call them now. We can't let the kidnappers have any more of a head start than they already have," Desireé says.

"Okay. First let me tell you about McGee and Ivory. McGee's full name is a mouthful: Joseph Patrick Aloysius Michael John McGee."

Desireé looks dubiously at her husband.

"I swear. That almost theatrical name was a gift from his mother—who was more Irish than the Fenians and more Catholic than the pope. She was very young when McGee was born and could not make up her mind what to call him; so, she used all the names from some little Irish song. Having such a peculiar name guaranteed that McGee would grow up tough—something on the order of being named 'Sue' like the Johnny Cash song. Like me, he learned to fight in the first grade and earned a crooked nose and the right to be known only as McGee to everyone but his mother after that.

"McGee became a private investigator in an unlikely way. Most PIs were former cops who either became unfit for further NYPD service or retired with a nice letter, a nice plaque, and a meager pension, and chose being a PI over being a security guard. McGee told me that he knew what he wanted to be from his midteens. He studied up on what it took to be a successful PI in a highly competitive market. Then he went after it. He got a degree in criminology at CUNY, graduating with honors after three years, and a law degree from Columbia. If I remember correctly, his first job was as a CSI for NYPD. That lasted three years, and then he quit because the pay was too low and the promotions too slow. Then he worked as a criminalist for the FBI specializing in ballistics and then banking fraud for a total of five years. On the QT, McGee said that he quit because he could no longer stomach the bureaucracy. PI work is not all that lucrative for most people, probably because they are just not suited for high-end work. His firm—McGee & Associates—does its share of nasty divorce dirt digging and embezzlement work and that stuff, but their real money comes from surveillance in corporate espionage cases, forensic accountancy, and in-depth investigations for the defense in high-profile criminal cases—usually murders, but the firm has helped more than a few parents whose children have been taken. They have a serious but not advertised reputation for being no-questions-asked investigators, negotiators, and rescuers.

"The office of McGee & Associates Investigations is in midtown Manhattan, is clean and presentable with chrome and glass fixtures, and no handpainted signs by the proprietor—another set of differences between McGee's and the lower class of PIs whom the real cops refer to as "bottom feeders." They don't advertise on TV or on billboards. Their clients are largely rich, have serious issues with opponents; or, in criminal cases, they have vices to hide and important secrets to keep. They are sticklers for ethics. We can talk with McGee or Ivory, and I'm sure you'll be impressed.

"Besides McGee himself, there are two other partners: Caitlin O'Brian, who has been with me for six months. Her former occupation was as one of New York's finest, a homicide detective in the Central Investigation and Resource Division, Homicide Analysis Unit, who ran afoul of her precinct captain. It seems that there was a disagreement about who had the right to do what with which and to whom, and she decked him. To avoid unpleasantness of separation with its attendant negative publicity, Catlin accepted a full pension and a nice letter of recommendation. She is a tough black Irish girl from the Bronx who had four brothers—a condition that lent itself to an early education in fighting. After finishing the academy and doing her rookie year, she obtained an associate degree in criminology specializing in bank fraud and handwriting analysis. That proved to be boring, so the feisty colleen moved to the homicide division of midtown Manhattan where McGee and Ivory first met her.

"You might have heard of Ivory White back when we worked together. We parted on good terms. Ivory White is a most unlikely name for the blackest man I ever met—even blacker than me. He has something of a murky past about which only McGee knows everything, and no one else but me knows anything. He's the muscle of the organization. He is tall, athletic, bald, arrogant, and mean if needs be—and that is often the case in his line of work, perhaps best known by its euphemism—'special investigations.' He does all of the serious personal security for high profile clients. For all of his martial arts and other physical skills sets, Ivory is extremely intelligent. He is a remarkable linguist who speaks six of the most useful languages of the 800 used by the citizens of the most densely populated city in the country if not the world. He is an extremely determined man. Nobody refuses him when he is sure he is on the right track."

"I'm convinced. Call him now, please, Damien."

He nods and picks up his iPhone.

"McGee & Associates Investigations," the receptionist answers.

"I need to speak to McGee or to Ivory White. It is urgent. Tell them it is Damien Markee, their Friday night friend.

"Yes, sir."

McGee answers after a short pause, "What's up, Damien?"

"Not on the phone, McGee. Please bring Ivory and come to room 1241 in the Carlyle. My wife and I need your help ASAP."

"We'll be there."

Chapter Five

"Come in McGee, Ivory," says Desireé.

"Damien? Desireé? What's up?"

"McGee, Ivory, I ... we need your help for a huge family problem."

"How can we be of help?"

"Our daughters, Paprika and Cinnamon, have been kidnapped. We got a ransom demand no more than ten minutes ago."

"I was watching WNN on the way over here. I didn't see an Amber Alert. This smacks of complications."

"That would make you the master of understatement, my friend. Let me give you the short version and ask you to get to work for us as fast as possible."

For the next half an hour, Damien and Desireé work as a team to fill in all of the details of the day thus far. Damien tells McGee and Ivory frankly why they cannot go to the police over and above the obvious fact that their daughters' kidnappers require them not even to hint to police anything about the incident.

"I don't need to tell you that I have enemies … more than I can count. That's why my wife and girls live separately and under assumed names. There are people around the city—especially in Harlem—who will not hesitate to take advantage of our turmoil. NYPD is full of corruption; I know that as well as anybody since I have a slew of them on my payroll. If the word gets out, there will be a frenzied attempt to find the girls and to steal them from the original kidnappers; so, they can up the ante."

"I don't know, Damien." says Ivory. "The NYPD and the FBI have good track records for getting children back, saving the ransom money, and getting convictions. Maybe you ought to involve them. The more boots on the ground, the better."

"What do you think about paying the ransom?" Desireé asks Ivory.

"From what I've read and experienced, paying or not paying is about a statistical toss-up. Neither law enforcement nor us can advise you on that. However, we should let some time pass and not appear to be too anxious. We'll need proof of life, exact information from the kidnappers about how the transfer of funds is to be accomplished, to do the best and most unobtrusive search we can do, and to rescue them if an opportunity arises."

"I want to be involved," says Damien.

"We can talk about that later, Damien, but for now hold tight and let us cover as much ground as possible before you make yourself a public target. We can talk more about that as things progress."

Damien gives a shrug of acquiescence but does not meet McGee eye-to-eye.

"I brought a contract for us to sign. We will need to talk about any developments immediately and at least a couple of times of day. That all right with you?"

Both Damien and Desireé agree.

McGee enters the conversation, "Damien, let me fill you in on how we work. Our policy is to provide the truth; and all clients who pay the bills are informed up front that we will not lie for them in or out of court; and we will give them all of what we discover and let them be the judge of how to use the information. We don't take bribes; anyone who does such a thing will be kicking rocks down the road half a minute after I learn that he or she does. Sometimes our clients balk at such pristine morality, but it has paid off over the two decades we have been in business. Let me ask a question: do we work for both of you?"

"Yes," Desireé says emphatically and gives her husband a determined look.

Damien nods his agreement.

"Okay. Ivory and I brought a box of burner phones. We will use them exclusively, or we will communicate face to face. Trust no one else. Use your usual landlines or cell phones or your e-mails, but keep all of those communications limited to routine daily business and chit chat. If the kidnappers are savvy about electronics and are accomplished hackers, they will be able to monitor everything you say. Someone from our firm will come by your homes in the wee hours of every night to sweep for listening devices, but we don't want to put in a scrambler on your phones or in any of the rooms of your house or businesses. That should reassure the kidnappers that you are complying with their demand to keep the police and the FBI entirely out of the effort. Your phones will have a recording device that will automatically feed our office any contact you get with the criminals. Don't try to be clever and to get them to linger longer than ordinary to allay their fears that calls are being traced.

"We have to presume that you two are in danger; so, Ivory and his surveillance team will be nearby wherever you are. The team is very discreet and has a perfect record for watching clients without being detected.

"One last thing before you get to ask questions. Our other partner, Caitlin O'Brian, is a first-class electronic communications genius. She will need full access to your e-mails, social media accounts, and your business data. We are absolutely discreet. In the past we have learned about criminal activities on the part of our clients. We provide the clients with what we learn and leave it at that. We never go behind our clients' backs and report to law enforcement."

Damien looks dubious but decides to hold his tongue for the time being.

"Questions?" McGee asks.

Desireé has one. "So, when does all of this get going?"

"As soon as you can get back home—your respective homes. From what the kidnappers said, they will likely be calling you, Mrs. Paxton. I think it is important for you to be available and for you to maintain your identity as Angelina Paxton and to keep your distance from Damien more than you have been doing in recent months. We don't know if money is the sole reason for the kidnapping; maybe it is somebody with a grudge against Damien or who is after leverage. We'll learn more when they make their next call."

The Chevy drives about for over an hour and the girls are aware that they are making many turns, including U turns. Getting car sick, Paprika vomits inside her hood and starts to choke. Cinnamon screams, and the car abruptly stops. The rear doors of the vehicle fly open and harsh voices yell at them. However, one of the abductors recognizes that Paprika is in trouble, maybe choking or suffocating. He rips off her hood and wipes her face with a garage towel, and the little girl is able to blow the vomitus from her nostrils and mouth. In a few minutes, her breathing returns to normal, and the ride resumes. After about half an hour, the car slows to a stop; and two strong men carry Cinnamon and Paprika into a building and remove their hoods and wrist and ankle bindings. The room is dark and the abductors remain shrouded in black clothes with nothing but eye slits showing. They leave the room, and the two sisters fall into each other's arms sobbing.

A few minutes later, the unmarked van pulls up to the building; and the girls' three security officers are roughly herded up a short flight of stairs, across a wood floor then up two flights of stairs. One of the abductors opens a heavy door and shoves Lydia and Chet into a room with no furniture.

"Sit," orders the kidnapper. "Don't say nothin' or you'll regret it a whole lot."

He removes the plastic wrist and ankle bindings then quickly leaves the room. Lydia and Chet hear the door slam and multiple locks being closed.

They wait five minutes, then Lydia whispers, "Chet?"

"Yeah," he whispers back.

"Andy?" No answer.

She asks again, and is again met with silence.

She listens carefully, then takes the risk and removes her hood, aware of the foul odor coming from the inner lining of the hood from sweat and fear. She is sure that not all of the odor is from her.

She looks around, and determining that she and Chet are alone, she moves to him and removes his hood.

The room is very dark, but the crack under the door and around the two windows lets in just enough light that the two imprisoned security guards can get an idea of the room where they are being held prisoner.

"Any idea what happened to Andy?" Lydia asks.

"He was in the van with us. They must have taken him someplace else in this building," Chet replies.

"That doesn't sound good," Lydia says.

"And probably isn't going to be good for you and me, either, Lydia," Chet says.

"Look, we need to get an idea what kind of place this is and how to get out of it," Lydia tells Chet.

"I agree. Why don't we feel around the floorboards and the windows to find out at least whether or not this is a house, or an old office building, or whatever."

They crawl on their hand and knees.

Chet is the first to find something.

"Feels like a bed pan and a hospital urinal," he says.

Lydia finds three trays with paper cups and plastic utensils on her side of the room. They meet at the window and find it's casings to be secured to the wall. The openings are closed over with slick painted two by two boards. The only thing they can ascertain about the outside world is that it must be daytime because of the thin but bright light coming in.

Desireé returns to her condominium at 142 West 129th Street and her identity as Angelina Paxton. Separately, Caitlin O'Brian and her number two, Grant Lathrum, meet McGee and Ivory at a Wendy's on Fredrick Douglass Boulevard. David Harger and his senior technical assistant, Craig Yankovich, and Caitlin's assistant, Rosalie Hertel, arrive in separate cars. After a brief conference, Harger, Yankovich, and Hertel drive to the unofficial BK office in the East Harlem Men's Club on 133rd Street. McGee, Ivory, Caitlin, and Grant drive to Angelina's neighborhood and park four blocks away from her condo. They split up and walk around blocks; so, they can all arrive at the back of the building at different times and from different directions.

Once in Angelina's condo, Caitlin and Grant set to work to place listening and recording devices on all phones—land and cell—Angelina's computer, and in strategic locations around the interior of the five-story residence and in the garage. After two hours work, she is satisfied and then sits down in front of Angelina's computer and—using Angelina's entry codes—is into the young mother's life from its every personal, social, and business avenue. She copies the hard drive; so, she can study its contents at her leisure back at the McGee & Associates offices over the next couple of days. She works a little magic and brings up a separate copy of all of Angelina's deleted material—millions of bytes worth. She knows she will be busy for four or five days total. Without Angelina's knowledge, Grant hacks into her business and social media files and harvests a crop of secrets that Angelina would not like Damien to know, but nothing that seems to be connected to or a motive for the kidnappings.

Damien meets David, Craig, and Rosalie at the Men's Club and drives them down the one-way street—Lexington Avenue—to his real office in Turtle Bay, east midtown Manhattan. They exit onto 42nd Street, and he parks in the private basement parking area of the Chrysler Building—a place he has scrupulously kept secret for the past decade of his career as the *capo di tutti capi*—or general—of the Black Knights. Damien and his guests travel on the inlaid wood-lined express elevator to his office on the 71st floor. The gilt sign on the plate glass door informs the visitor that these are the offices of Turtle Bay Investment Fund Managers, Inc.

Damien leads them down a hardwood floor hallway overlain with hand knotted Chinese silk runners past offices indicating the name of the occupant and his or her title. At the far end of the hallway, they come to the only door that has no glass. It is a solid and ornate mahogany work of art. Near the doorknob is a three by four-inch brass plate that reads simply, "CEO." Only after the four enter the palatial skyscraper office with a view of the Hudson River on the west and a small portion of the Harlem River on the east, does he speak.

"Okay, you have access to this computer in my office and only this one. You are getting to see into my secret business here only because I trust Ivory White and McGee completely. Nothing you learn here ever gets talked about outside of the very, very few people who need to know. You have this privilege because my two little daughters have been stolen, and I will turn over heaven and earth to get them back. I am not a nice man. I think you already know that. The consequences for any of this information you pick up getting out, especially to my … competitors … or the police would be … to put it delicately … drastic."

Damien's face has that chiseled-in-stone visage that must have been on the face of *Ozymandias* as described by Percy Bysshe Shelley: whose frown, and wrinkled lip, and sneer of cold command … and on the pedestal these words appear—"My name is Ozymandias, king of kings: look on my works, ye Mighty, and despair." David, Craig, and Rosalie get the message and each have a brief inward shiver. Working for McGee has its distinct benefits, but some of the characters they deal with cause them to doubt their choice of employment from time to time.

He leaves the three computer experts to their work. They make a deep personal promise not to remember Damien's passwords once they leave the Chrysler Building. By midnight, they have information they think might be useful. Damien had very recently been in a meeting with several of the crime syndicate leaders with whom he was plotting a treaty to recognize criminal enterprise territories and to respect them. Disrespect of the contractual arrangements could be a capital crime they learn. They also learn that the Genovese family refuses to meet with Damien—a racist show of disrespect that Damien has no intention of forgetting. He has assigned Alphonso Vergansi, his only Italian underboss, to find out for sure who is the elusive boss of bosses of the Genoveses. He also called a man named Hector "Ice-man" Aguilara in Los Angeles and paid for a first-class plane trip for the man to come to Harlem.

There is no information on this computer about legitimate business. The other business described in the electronic folders is difficult to decipher because it is presented in heavily colloquial language with the frequent use of idioms of the black underworld. The gist of the records is evident: "Hos" followed by a listing of areas with a few definite addresses in one column and a number in a second column adds up to more than ten million a month. The addresses include locations in almost every city in the United States and Canada with a population over 200,000. "Fun &" is a more obscure heading and its addresses are fewer—limited to the largest cities in the country. The numbers column adds up to more than a hundred million, but the numbers are declining by about ten or fifteen percent every year for the past ten years.

Rosalie says, "The numbers rackets," and her coworkers agree.

Another column is headed, "The Law." There are three columns and twelve rows: the first column is a ten-digit number, presumably a telephone number; the second column is a first name; and the third column is a very succinct descriptor such as "reliable," "a bit crazy," "spooky and unpredictable," "good at short notice," and "woman." The twelve rows have only sets of mixed numbers, letters, and computer signs with a total of fifteen characters each; for example, the second row is 12/12/92 ☺ §HIA_w. McGee's computer experts are sure that the obtuse identifiers are computer logins for a select group of individuals, but no one without a list of the names associated with the apparently random groupings of numbers, letters, and symbols could use the information.

Craig sums up what they all presume, "Hit men."

Chapter Six

"Are the bad men gone, Cinnamon?" Paprika asks her big sister.

"I think so, Paprika," Cinnamon answers.

"Where are we?"

"I don't know, but I think it's a house; and we are locked in one of the bedrooms."

The room is moderately well lit by fluorescent lighting from behind the base boards below and from a cornice projecting out from the top of the beige-colored walls above. The girls make a quick inspection. The room is not quite as expensively decorated as their rooms at home, but it is a reasonably nice prison. The floor is carpeted wall-to-wall with a plush beige-colored carpet that has multiple spots of half a dozen different colors. There is a bright red round table with two small brightly painted chairs. On the table are coloring books, crayons, colored pencils, and an assortment of highlighters. There is a queen-size bed covered with a brightly patterned duvet, a Barbie Doll set, and a plush fuzzy teddy bear, toys and books on the bedside tables, and a medium-sized bathroom with twin sinks, a shower, and a bathtub. There are separate piles of fluffy large towels. The closet in the bedroom is empty of clothing but has several dozen clothes hangers.

There are indications on the wall that a large window was once there but has been removed and plastered over. There is no doorknob on the only door granting entrance and exit from the room. There are no locks on the door from the inside. Cinnamon pushes on the door, but it does not move a millimeter. She knocks on it and hears a metallic sound behind the thin wood façade. She attempts to squeeze her small fingers under the door, but the space is too tight.

"You try, Paprika. Your fingers are smaller."

She tries, but even her little girl fingers are too thick.

"Are we going to be here forever, Cinnamon?" the younger sister asks with a quavering voice trying not to cry any more.

"No, little sister. We are going to find a way out. We'll find a place where we can knock a hole in the wall and crawl through, or we'll trick the bad men and sneak around them."

The suggestion sounds as ridiculous as it is, but just the mental gymnastics of trying to find a way to escape is therapeutic.

"We can bash the guy who brings us food and steal his keys. That's what Daddy would do ... but he's big and tough, and we are little and weak," Paprika says, and gives in to a few tears that cannot be restrained.

Cinnamon gives her a hug.

"I'm hungry," Paprika says. "Do you think they are going to let us starve?"

"I don't. There is some reason why we are being kept in a nice room; so, I'll bet we get decent food. For now—until we can figure out what to do to escape—I think we should pretend to cooperate; so, they don't get mad at us."

"Okay for now. But when I get a chance, I am going to kick one of them in the place were boys hate to get kicked."

Both little girls begin to laugh.

Upstairs in their bleak dark room, Lydia and Chet are plotting their escape on a more serious level.

"Can anything in the trays or plates or cups be made into a shiv?" Chet asks.

"It's all pretty innocuous stuff—paper and flimsy plastic. I think our martial arts skills are going to be more effective weapons," Lydia answers.

"You're right, Lydia. I might add that our brains are more likely to prove to be the best weapons. We need to brainstorm about how we go about tricking and overpowering the guy who feeds us. Speaking of which, what I wouldn't give for a great artery-hardening cheeseburger and a pile of curly fries."

"Now that you mention it, I'm getting pretty hungry myself. They took our watches; so, I can hardly even guess what time it is. It seems like we've been in here for two months."

"More like two hours, but I don't fault your guesswork."

Lydia becomes thoughtful.

"Chet, I think the first thing we have to do is to learn as much as we can about where we are, what kind of a place this is, and what kind of people we are dealing with."

Chet slides his hands around on the walls to see if there is a light switch, not really expecting to find one. His expectations are met. Lydia taps the walls—more accurately percusses the walls—like a doctor doing a chest examination, listening to an indication of a hollow spot where maybe there is nothing but wallboards separating an empty space between them. After ten minutes at her task, she gets the hang of it and finds that she can determine when she is tapping over a two-by-four upright framing board and when she is in the space between them. She covers most of the room in the next fifteen minutes and decides that there is nothing special about the wall construction—no sounds coming back from the percussion to indicate metal or board paneling.

Chet says, "So, maybe if we can choose the right time when the kidnappers are not right in the next room, we can employ those vaunted karate kicks of ours and punch a hole through the wall."

"I think that is a real possibility, partner," Lydia says. "After all, mean drunks and wife beaters do it all the time. That's where the brain part is going to have to come into play. We have got to learn their routine; so, we can attack the wall at a time when it won't be so obvious."

"Oh, yeah," says Chet, "so we don't get our brains blown out."

"Speaking of that, what do you think has happened to Andy? The poor guy's first day on the job, he gets abducted by a bunch of thugs; and nobody knows where he is."

"Or whether he is even still alive," Chet says angrily.

The condo phone rings, and Angelina gets up quickly to answer it.

"Let it ring twice more before you answer, Angelina," says Caitlin. "It is better not to have them think you are too anxious."

The phone chimes again.

"You need to demand proof of life but tell them the deal's off if they harm the girls in any way. Tell them your husband agrees."

The phone chimes the third time.

"Hello," answers Angelina slightly breathlessly.

"Hey, broad, what kept you? You think this some some kinda little game you rich girls get to play?"

Caitlin, McGee, Ivory, and Grant are listening to every word via the connections Caitlin and Grant made an hour before.

"I was in the bathroom," Angelina lies without a trace of guile in her voice.

Caitlin says to herself, *This girl is a good actress; it looks like she will be able to rise to the occasion.*

"Awright. Next time sit on the phone."

"I will. How are my girls?"

"We'll get to that in a coupla minutes. First, I'm gonna lay out what you—just you—are gonna do and when to pay the ransom. The kids are fine, by the way."

"We have…."

"Stuff a sock in it until I finish with the instructions. This is how it's gonna go down: you will obtain twenty-five million dollars in bearer bonds called Baklava bonds obtained in high denominations of Turkish lira [TL] issued by Finans Bank Anonim Şirketi. The bank's simpler trade name is 'Finansbank.' The company's head office is in Istanbul. Now write this down: its address is "Büyükdere Cad. No: 129 Mecidiyeköy." You will have to make the purchase initially in euros from Deutsche Bank in Bonn and then use the euros to purchase the Turkish bearer bonds. Do you understand what I have just said?"

"Not a word," Angelina says. "Tell me the name of the bank in Turkey and whatever a bear bond is."

"It is called a bearer bond. B-E-A-R-E-R," said the machine-distorted phone voice, sounding irritated and as if it were speaking to a slow child; but it repeated the difficult Turkish names.

"I'll make it simple," the kidnapper continued. "Bearer bonds became for all practical purposes illegal in the United States in 1982, but they are still legal in many other countries. A bearer bond is a debt security—a formal legal document which is redeemable just like money, no questions asked. The bonds are issued by a business entity, such as a corporation like the Finansbank, or by a government. The Turkish bearer bond we want differs from the more common types of investment securities in that it is unregistered; no records are kept of the owner or the transactions involving ownership. Whoever physically holds the paper—namely me—for which the bond is issued, owns the instrument. This is useful for investors who wish to retain anonymity—so you see why we want to go this way."

"I guess so. I have no idea how to go about this, though," Angelina says.

"You're a smart lady: use your iPhone. Transfer funds from your account or accounts to the Deutsche Bank in Bonn and talk to one of the savvy bankers there and give him instructions to be ready to accept your funds. To ensure speed and safety, we require you—and you alone—to carry out the transaction in Istanbul and to take physical possession of the actual bearer bonds.

"In one week I will make another call to tell you how the transfer of the bearer bonds for the children will be carried out."

The kidnapper's telephone clicked off.

"We still didn't get proof of life," McGee says. "The next time you talk to the kidnappers, Angelina, you must insist on that."

"What should I do about the ransom?"

"It is decision time. I think we should use a burner phone and call Damien to share in the decision. It is his money that will be used, I presume?"

"Yes. I'll make the call."

Five minutes and three attempts later, Damien answers his throw-away mobile phone.

"I presume this is important," he says.

"Damien," Angelina says, "the kidnappers called with ransom demand details."

"I'm sorry you had to deal with that, Desireé."

Damien is highly and persistently resistant to calling his wife by her assumed name in private.

"What do they want?"

"You know about the twenty-five million dollars. They want us to pay them with something called bearer bonds from a bank in Turkey. They demand that I go alone to Istanbul and take care of the arrangements personally. First, we would have to make a wire transfer from your account to the Deutsche Bank in Bonn in euros. The bank will make the transfer to the Turkish bank, and then I will go and get the physical papers … the bonds … themselves. I don't know how to get them back to the United States. That will be a lot of bulk to try and get on flight back here. I think there are laws about how much money you can bring into the country."

"Ten thousand dollars. The plane won't be a problem. I have a contract with a private jet corporation; so, you can fly back and forth without any customs problems. What we need to decide right now is whether or not to pay the ransom. Do we have proof of life?"

"No, the kidnapper gave the instructions almost as fast as he could talk then hung up."

"Was McGee able to trace the call?"

"Too brief."

"That puts us between a rock and a hard place. What does McGee think about paying the ransom?"

"I'll have to ask him. Hang on a minute."

Angelina turns to McGee who has been listening on the speakerphone.

McGee says, "The FBI says don't pay. Statistics are very hard to come by; but the evidence does not support benefit from paying a ransom for what is called a 'stereotypical' kidnapping—that is, an abduction of a child by a nonfamily stranger. In an average year about 115 such kidnappings take place in the US; the rest of the more than 58,000 kidnappings are family related."

Angelina interrupts, "But does paying the ransom make the chances of recovery of the child or children—as in our case—more or less likely? What are the chances that we'll get our children back, anyway?"

"Apparently, ransom payment in stereotypical kidnappings is not better than refusing to pay. I hate to answer your second question; but unfortunately, forty percent of such kidnapped children are murdered, and four percent are lost without information ever being discovered about what happened to them. For your insight, the FBI says that parents only contact police in about twenty percent of cases of kidnapping."

Angelina starts to cry.

Damien says, "I have something to say on the subject that might make a difference."

"What?" demands Angelina.

"A few years ago, I took out kidnapping and ransom insurance on myself, you, Desireé, and Cinnamon and Paprika. I also included three of my top business associates. When I did that, the insurance broker told me to keep it a secret because knowledge of the insurance by the kidnapped person might cause him or her to act differently and to endanger himself and my company even more. The insurance guy told me that there are cases where having such knowledge has led to the victim colluding with the kidnappers. More often than not, such victims are murdered to hide the facts."

"And you didn't tell me!" Angelina snarls, unable to control her anger. "That settles it once and for all. We are going to pay the ransom. It is the only thing we can control in this whole terrible mess. Damien, you must not deny my request to save our children. I would never recover, and I would never forgive you if you let them die for failure to part with the money. You have tons of it."

"Damien," McGee asks, "how much insurance do you have?"

"Fifty million."

"The premiums must be a king's ransom."

"They are, and I guess this is the time to cash in. I'll make the arrangements with the insurance company."

"Will they honor the demand to avoid police?" Angelina asks.

"It's part of the insurance agreement. They make no demands other than proof that the named victims have actually been abducted."

"If you two are in agreement, we have several things to demand of the kidnappers when they call next. We have to have proof of life and a handwritten ransom demand note to take to the insurance company. We can alert the insurance company to have the funds ready for the wire transfer to Bonn, but we probably shouldn't actually make the transfer until the kidnappers keep their end of the deal."

"I agree," says Damien.

Angelina softly gives her consent then goes into her bedroom and locks the door.

Chapter Seven

It is day two of the kidnapping of Cinnamon and Paprika Paxton—Chet Nichols, Andy Lusesky, and Lydia Fairchild, security guards from the private company, New York Protection Service, missing with them.

Chet and Lydia have not heard anything in the past several hours suggesting that the kidnappers are still in the building where they are being held prisoner. Nor have they learned anything concerning the whereabouts of the two little girls for whom they have responsibility to protect or of their fellow security officer, Andy Lusesky. It is time to take a chance. They have determined that one area of the wall in their prison room sounds more hollow, and, therefore, more vulnerable.

"Let's do it," Chet says.

"Okay. On three," Lydia says. "You go first."

Chet gives the wall a powerful karate back kick and drives his foot into the drywall panel. Neither he nor Lydia harbor any illusions that the kick would not be heard if anyone is still in the building beyond the wall, and the noise of his kick rivals the decibels of a shotgun blast. Lydia takes her turn, using a straight front kick that widens the area of damage to the wall. The noise of her kick is equally loud. Chet gives her a high-five. He backs up to get a little running room for his next kick just as the only door to the room flies open. Six men dash into the room and take down Lydia and Chet after a one minute struggle. One of the kidnappers brings in two stiff back metal chairs with arm rests, and the two captives are jammed into the chairs with sufficient force to jar their spines and to bruise their coccyx bones.

The captors bind Lydia and Chet's wrists and ankles to the chairs and slap duct tape over their eyes and mouths. Then, they are systematically beaten with a small-size baseball bat over their calves, their thighs, their backs, and their arms.

"You wanna stay alive?" the machinelike voice asks, and Chet and Lydia nod in the affirmative.

"You get a day to sit here hungry and thirsty to ponder your sins and your choices for the future. Do what you have to do about excretion. It was your choice to violate the rules, and you can sit around in your own stink as a result."

The pain in their throbbing contused muscles is severe, but they are surprised even to be alive. Both personal security guards have decidedly started considering the option that efforts to escape are futile and likely to be the cause of them being killed. The world looks bleak.

Cinnamon is tired, angry, frightened, and working herself up to one of her explosions that her anger management counselor has been working for two years to get the headstrong girl to avoid. She tries to think of something else. She sings a little Jesus song from her Sunday school class at the AME [African Methodist Episcopalian] on Amsterdam Avenue. It does not help.

The masked captor pushes open the door to the bedroom where Cinnamon and Paprika are being held captive. The captor is carrying a supper tray in each hand and is being careful not to tip over the trays and make a mess. Cinnamon decides this is her chance.

She whispers to Paprika, "When I kick him, you run out the door and get to the street. This could be our only chance."

Paprika whimpers but says she'll try.

Cinnamon works up a head of steam and propels herself into the midsection of the captor who is struggling to maintain the balance of the trays. The eleven-year-old girl crashes her head in a nearly perfect spear block move into the most vulnerable part of the captor who screams, surprising both little girls and the female captor. The woman topples over unable to get her breath, and scatters food and utensils all around the previously neat bedroom.

Cinnamon shrieks at Paprika, "Get outta here! Run, girl, run!"

Paprika breaks out of her state of shock at what Cinnamon has done and makes a beeline for the door, which is still partway open. She finds herself alone in a wide carpeted hallway leading both left and right. She is left handed; so, she automatically makes the decision to run in that direction. It turns out to be a good choice because the stairs are located there, and she is able to get to them and down two flights before anyone reacts to the pandemonium going on in the girls' bedroom. She can see the front door of the house twenty yards away, across an open slate rock floor foyer.

Cinnamon jumps up from the floor where she lands beside the captor who is still fighting to breathe and charges for the door which is almost closed.

The woman croaks out a command, "Stop, you little devil; or I'll whup yoah backside until y'all cain't set fa a week!"

It comes out so weak and breathy that it is almost comical, and Cinnamon pays her no mind. She dashes into the hall and turns right. At the corner of the hallway is an L-shaped dead-end, and she has to reverse direction and run back the way she came. She passes the door to the bedroom just as the woman kidnapper opens it and steps out on wobbly legs. The woman makes an attempt to grab the fleeing girl but it is too-little-too-late, and the athletic child streaks for the stairs at the other end of the hall. She takes the stairs two at a time and makes it down one flight before running into two large men who have not had time to put on their ski masks. One is white and the other is black. As the brutes take her down, she has the odd feeling she has seen the white man before. In two minutes she is back in her bedroom, trussed up, and lying on the bed.

The woman kidnapper is able to breathe now, and she tells Cinnamon, "I'll get y'all, an' ya gonna regret what y'all done fa a week, baby gull!"

But for the moment, she has to join the other four kidnappers as they rush out of the house and onto the street to recapture Paprika. Paprika is smart enough to know that she cannot outrun the adults for long. She has three advantages over her captors: she has a three-minute head start; she is small; and she is smart. She has no idea where she is except that it is a residential neighborhood of stand-alone houses with large backyards. She rounds a block, then turns onto the next street going away from the kidnap house. She turns her head just enough to determine that her pursuers are not in sight. Then she ducks down a brick driveway and into a backyard with a lot of apple and peach trees, shrubs, cute little doghouses, and Disney character statues—exactly her kind of place. She runs behind a hedge and wedges herself

onto the ground of a flower patch nestled among small syca-
more trees and makes herself as small as she can. Her heart is
thumping out of her chest, and her breath sounds to her like
a steam locomotive.

The kidnappers run out of the house in a tightly packed
group of five in what is beginning to look like a proverbial
Chinese fire drill. The white man who helped recapture
Cinnamon takes charge.

"We have to stop calling attention to ourselves. An adult
man running after a child in this neighborhood will bring
cops from every direction in a matter of minutes. Anyone
have any idea which direction she ran?"

The problem for the kidnappers is that the house they are
using as a prison is located in the middle of the block. Paprika
could have run left or right and then turned left or right when
she got to the corner. The first permutation of directions is
a factor of four, and there are only five of them to conduct
a search with a dual goal of finding and recapturing the girl
and not drawing the attention of neighbors and police.

"Everybody got a cell phone on them?" the white man asks
the four African-American kidnappers.

They nod.

"Okay, everybody split up into twos and go to the end of
the block and then split up again. Keep in cell phone contact
with everybody. If you find her, don't get out on a street with
a flailing and struggling child. Call for help. We'll search for
thirty minutes, then come back and get into cars and start a
grid search by car. I don't need to tell you how crucial it is
that we get that brat back unharmed and without us being
seen. Think life in prison if this goes any more south than it
already has. Now, let's get going."

Damien switches his burner phone to off after his conversation with McGee. He checks his business phone book on his regular iPhone and finds the number for his insurance agent, who happens to be a close associate in the rackets and very aware of Damien's business.

"Hey, Damien, whus up?"

"Hey, Phoenix. Got a big time problem which involves you."

"I'm all ears."

"This doesn't go beyond us two ... nobody else, even family, the guys we trust the most, or anywhere close to cops."

"Sounds pretty much like business as usual."

"Believe me, it's not."

"Is this a K&R insurance matter, bro?"

"Yes."

"You on a secure phone?"

"A burner."

"I'm not. I got your phone number ID. I'll get my own burner, never used, and call you right back."

Three long minutes pass.

"Hey, Damien."

"Okay, Phoenix. This is the long and short of it: my two baby girls have been kidnapped, and the fools that took 'em are demanding twenty-five mil by a week from now."

"Whew."

"Yeah. They have a good plan. No cops; they only deal with Desireé. I'm not sure they even know her fake name."

"I don't even know that."

"I guess it's time you did. She's living under the name of Angelina Paxton with my two daughters, Cinnamon and Paprika. The girls were abducted yesterday afternoon."

"Those cute little spices. We'll turn over heaven and earth to get them back."

"Not yet. I have McGee and Ivory White on it. They are as discreet and effective as you can get. They are handling a lot of the details."

"I'll get you the money, but you know these things take time."

"How much time?"

"Depends. Could be as much as a couple of weeks."

"The kidnappers told Desireé they'd kill the kids if we don't comply. We have a week."

"I'll give it my best shot, bro. How's it supposed to go down?"

"The insurance comes up with the money. The kidnappers don't need to know that or how much the coverage really is. Then, the money gets wire-transferred to Deutsche Bank in Bonn, Germany. I guess Desireé will have to go to Bonn to get the next step underway."

"Which is?"

"Funds transfer to an Istanbul, Turkey bank called Finansbank. They create bearer bonds which Desireé brings back to New York in time to give them to the kidnappers, and we get our girls back."

"You sure about this, Damien? I mean, I don't want to bring up nasty stuff, but the fibbies never advise parents to pay. It don't work. And bearer bonds? I think they are pretty much illegal, aren't they?"

"In the United States, bearer bonds have historically been the financial instrument of choice criminals like me and you for money laundering, tax evasion, and other concealed business transactions. In response, new issuances of bearer bonds have been severely curtailed in the United States since 1982. I did a bit of research and learned that in the United States all the bearer bonds issued by the US Treasury have matured. They no longer pay interest to the holders. Those outstanding can still be cashed in at face value, but there are very few left. However, other countries still issue them or allow their private financial institutions to do so. The Turkish government encourages foreign investment, and has a Foreign Direct Investment Law with implementing rules that have eliminated most restrictions on foreign investors and granted them the same legal status as Turkish companies under the Commercial Code. The important thing about Turkey and countries like it that allow bearer bonds is that their bonds have to be honored at any nation's banking institution which recognizes its money. They have what they call the Capital Markets Law. It allows—and, in fact—encourages investors to purchase and sell all kinds of capital market instruments, including all types of securities—State Partnership Bonds, bearer bonds, state issued securities, and to establish mutual funds. All of these create a system which protects investors who want to deal in bearer bonds without having to be registered or to give a reason for their purchase like the US requires. The Turkish State will—if necessary—act as an intermediary in the purchase and sale of such securities.

"The Turkish lira is fully convertible, at least from the Turkish side, because the country is recognized by the IMF as having achieved article 8 status."

"So, what's article 8?"

"I even wrote it down. Under article 8, 'no limitation may be imposed on the buying and selling of foreign exchange within the scope of current items in the balance of payments. Profits from these transactions must be freely convertible.' That is to say, Turkish bearer bonds are legal, and the guy who has one can turn it in for cash in almost every developed country. Obviously, there are countries—like Italy, Portugal, and Spain—that are not so uptight about it."

"I presume that means the kidnappers can disappear with their untraceable bearer bonds, cash them in, and sit around on the beach under the swaying palm tree and drink mint juleps or mai tais for the rest of their days."

"Um hmmh, that's it if we can't get witnesses or snitches who can get us an identity to look for."

"I can get the money PDQ because the insurance arrangements presume the potential for just such an emergency, I'm pretty sure."

"Get it. Put it into a readily available and usable account, but don't turn it over to us yet. We have to hear from the kidnappers first, and they have to give us proof of life before we can go any further. I think the girls are too valuable to them to cause them harm or to kill them, at least intentionally; so, I think they will do it within the next seven days. Then Desireé will head off to Germany and then to Turkey to get the bonds in hand. The transfer arrangements will probably be pretty complicated and dicey, but we'll cross that bridge when we come to it."

Chapter Eight

Paprika calms down over the next hour after finding the backyard hiding place. She knows she has to keep absolutely quiet and still. She establishes a simple plan: once it gets dark, she will come out of hiding and sneak around until she finds a house with people in it she can see, preferably a family. She will knock on the door and tell him she is the little girl they are talking about on the TV and the internet. Simple.

She hears a friendly voice calling her name, "Paprika. Paprika. Are you there? I'm a friend. Your mommy sent me to pick you up. I need to help you get away from the bad men."

Paprika starts to get up; but in the past two days, she has lost a great deal of her trusting nature; so, she listens. Nobody seems to be in the yard where she is. She hates to think that she will miss someone coming to save her. It is tempting to yell back, but she resists.

"Paprika, honey, I'm here to help. Your mommy sent me. If you can hear me, come over to where I am."

It can't hurt to investigate, can it?

She lifts her head and looks over the fence. There is no one in the yard with her. The voice must be coming from the sidewalk by the house. She crawls super quietly to the wide entrance into the backyard, keeping inside the flower beds and by shrubs and trees. The voice calls out again but is obviously getting farther away. She wants so much for it to be someone who can get her back home. Maybe he already has helped Cinnamon. She begins to hope.

Now, the voice is getting quite a ways away. She decides to take a chance. She hurries out to the edge of the trees in front of the house and sees the back of a man walking away.

"Paprika. I'm Uncle Kenny. Your mommy, Angelina, sent me. If you can hear me, and you are hiding, come out. We have to hurry, or the bad men will catch up to us."

It is too enticing, too genuine sounding; so, Paprika cautiously sneaks up the block behind front yard hedges until she is directly across from "Uncle Kenny." The hedge is eight feet tall and completely opaque to anyone looking in, but Paprika can push her face far enough in to make out the dim figure of the man who is making the siren call to her.

"I'm Paprika," she says in a voice only slightly above her usual conversational level.

The man stops dead in his tracks and swivels his head around to try and determine the direction from which the voice is coming.

"Sorry, I couldn't hear you very well," he says. "Please. Are you Paprika?"

"Yes," the little girl says, a little louder this time.

He hears her but is not entirely certain where she is. He cannot see anything that indicates her location.

"Come out; so, we can hurry away. My car is just two streets down and is waiting for us. We can't wait around. They're coming."

"What's the password?" Paprika asks.

She remembers what her mommy told her and that it would let her know if a man was trying to trick her.

"I...I...I forgot. Your mommy told me, but I just can't remember. Give me a hint. We can make it like a game, honey."

"You're a liar," Paprika calls out, quite a bit louder this time, forgetting the crucial need to hide in her excitement.

The password is "snow flake," and the man does not have a clue. Paprika is doing what her mother taught her to do in their fun but serious drills. She is running full out like a gazelle being chased by a determined leopard.

This time the man zones in on Paprika's voice with laser beam accuracy, and he runs towards the hedge. Paprika runs back the way she came as fast as her young legs can carry her. Two yards down the hedge is much lower, and she has to crawl. She hears the man trying to get through the gates of the yards where she has been. The gates are locked. He curses. When he gets to the yard with the lower hedge, he jumps over and runs back to where Paprika's voice came from. She runs into the shrubbery and flower beds of one more yard and then back into the yard where she spent the several hours hiding. Now, she can hear the man running towards her.

"Stop, little girl! I can see you. You can't get away. I won't hurt you. I'm your friend."

He is only ten yards behind her. Paprika has two advantages over the man. She knows the topography of that backyard as well as she knows her own bedroom, and she is much smaller than the man.

"Liar!" she yells and does a log roll under the masonry wall on the far side of the backyard a few seconds before his large hand can grab her. The wall is too high even to jump up and hold onto the top, and the opening at the bottom is barely high enough to admit the child, let alone the large, powerfully built man.

He flattens out on the ground, but can only see about a foot under the wall and knows that he has missed her. It is futile to run back out of the yard because he does not know which way she ran. Besides, he is now becoming keenly aware that the attention of the neighbors is surely going to be attracted to a large man running after a small girl. This is not the kind of neighborhood where that is acceptable behavior.

He gets smart and dials the group set on his cell phone.

"Found her," he says, "but she got away."

"Where are you? Or better, any idea where she is?" the lead kidnapper asks.

There is a pregnant pause.

"I dunno. I been chasin' the brat and lost track of the streets. Gimme a minute. I'll go check."

Five full minutes go by.

"Corey Way and Digis Street. Northwest corner."

"Wait there. We'll have three cars there in maybe ten minutes."

Angelina gets a burner phone message from Damien with the news that the money will be wire-transferred within the hour.

"I'll have to have my guys set up an emergency account in the Deutsche Bank Bonn, then we'll wire the money to that account as soon as we have proof of life. It'll be terrible, but we'll have to wait. We have to be certain, Desireé. I wish I could be with you through this. Are McGee and Ivory still with you?"

"Yes. We'll just wait here. Damien... I'm really scared for our girls."

"Me, too. I'm sure we'll find them. The money means nothing other than serving as a means of getting them back."

At two a.m., while Paprika lies hiding in another yard and feeling weak from hunger and thirst, Angelina gets a call that automatically goes to the speakerphones held by McGee, Ivory, and now, Caitlin O'Brian.

"This Mrs. Paxton?" the phony voice asks

It is something like Bogey talking to Ingrid Bergman.

"Yes."

"Here's what you need to know when you get to Bonn, and that can't be any later than tomorrow night."

Desireé is flustered but keeps her head, "Just you wait a minute. How do I even know that my little girls are with you or even alive?"

Her voice breaks a little.

"Just get the moola, sweetheart, and you'll get the girls back."

"Are they all right?"

"Peachy."

Then Desireé again remembers what she must have from the kidnappers, "I demand proof of life, or there will never be a ransom. We'll take our chances."

"What? Like you want us to cut off a pinkie finger or one of their ears? That what you have in mind?"

"Absolutely not. Get me an iPhone photo of both girls hold the morning edition of the *Times*. It has to be clear enough that I can see the headline."

"Do you have any idea what time it is, Lady?"

"I most certainly do, and I also know that the morning edition is out on the streets now. Send one of your goons out to get a front page. You can e-mail it with a burner phone to my cell-phone number: +1-917-223-6475," which indicates that it is a new number and almost certainly a disposable phone.

Paprika is cold, frightened, and now very hungry. She is exhausted; and, even at her tender age, she realizes she is too tired to run or fight or anything physical. It is very dark out. She knows she will have to go to sleep on the ground someplace, or she will have to knock on someone's door and take her chances. What if there are bears out at night? Or big spiders? Or zombies? Vampires come out at night. She knows that from TV. She starts to cry. Her fear of zombies and vampires trumps her worries about knocking on some stranger's door, even if it might be a mean man who hurts little girls. She cries harder, but she forces her weary little body up and starts out to find a nice looking house. They are all dark, and she has no idea which door to knock on. After a left and a right turn, she spies a house with a light on in an upstairs room. Maybe somebody is awake in there. Maybe it is a nice lady.

She looks all around. No vampires. No zombies. It is not very cold; so, there probably aren't any ghosts out tonight, at least in this part of town. She does not see any cars driving around or mean men out walking. She screws up all of her courage and walks up the sidewalk towards the front porch crying all the way.

Before she gets there, two black vehicles come from out of nowhere; and two men jump out of each car. Paprika's mind is dull from fear, hunger, thirst, and a feeling of hopelessness. She freezes and stands there with her head down. The men throw a hood over her head and throw her into the backseat of one of the big black cars. Upstairs in the house someone leans out the window and shouts.

"Stop! I see you! You have that little girl. I'm calling the police!"

The two cars burn strips of rubber on the asphalt and flee the neighborhood at breakneck speed with screeching tires, squealing brakes, and roaring engines. This excites more neighborhood interest and shortly, four 9-1-1 calls alert police. A preliminary Amber Alert is immediately put out and cell phones all over the city begin to ring and to vibrate. An APB and a BOLO hit the police communications system as fast as the dispatchers can type the information, skimpy as it is.

A fleet of police sedans screeches to a stop and blocks off the neighborhood. Cops leap out and begin a rapid response search on foot. Detectives interview all four 9-1-1 callers but get no really useful information—only that there were two SUVs, both dark in color, and nobody saw a license plate. Not surprisingly, the initial search is fruitless; so, the units regroup and begin a methodical gridiron drive around search of a ten-block area. The area is expanded to twenty blocks by first light and city and state wide by ten in the morning, but nothing turns up.

At 4:52, Desireé's burner rings again. There is a text from +1-646-288-4966 with a link but no caller ID. Desireé clicks on the link, and Caitlin's magic displays the attached digital photograph. McGee looks intently at Desireé although he is already almost certain it is of the Paxton girls. They are holding a *New York Times* front page with the headline, "PUTIN INVADES THE UKRAINE." Caitlin checks CNN on her iPhone and confirms that they are looking at today's early morning edition of the *Times*. Both Paxton girls are holding the paper, and both are obviously crying. Big hands are holding them roughly. There is no message, particularly, no instructions.

Desireé sobs.

McGee puts his arm around her shoulder, "Angelina, take this as good news. We know they are alive and neither of them looks like she has been hurt."

Caitlin adds, "And we know that they are in the Upper East Side with that +646 number."

Ivory says, "I'm on it. I'll get my homies out and cover the whole area. We all have such dark faces that the kidnappers will have no idea who's looking for them. Maybe they're white guys, and all us black folks look alike."

McGee says, "More like, 'in the dark, all cats are grey.' So, all you cats get out there. Let's find us two little girls!"

Chapter Nine

4:55 a.m. The kidnappers' safe house becomes animated like an African killer beehive under attack. Two men back the SUVs onto the lawn and leave the engines running and all doors open. Another two abductors rush into the dark room where the two security guards have been sitting handcuffed to stiff backed chairs for hours. The kidnappers release the leg bindings and jerk them upright. Chet cries out in pain from his back; and his partner, Lydia, crumples to the floor. Her cramped legs will not hold her up yet. Both of them receive several hard kicks and force themselves to become upright.

"Better!" growls the kidnapper. "Move out! NOW!"

Lydia Fairchild and Chet Nichols from the New York Protection Service stumble along as best they can on legs as stiff as new brooms.

Lydia knows she will regret it, but she asks anyway, "Where's our guy, Andy Lusesky? We have to know. He's our partner. Be a human being."

"Shut up!" the abductor says by way of response and gives each of them a backhand slap across the face.

He pushes the two security guards down the stairs and into the SUV on the right and shoves them into the backseat. He pushes the childproof locks and sits in the shotgun seat ready to leave.

A minute later, Cinnamon and Paprika Paxton are frog-walked to the SUV on the left and lifted bodily into the backseat and the childproof locks are engaged. The large vehicles pull out into the street and turn in opposite directions out of the neighborhood of the safe house. It is 5:22 a.m.

At 8:45 a.m., they meet in the parking area in the rear of a slum neighborhood and move their captives at the double into a two-story walk-up apartment—a dump. The Paxton girls are now in a room they would be unhappy to make their dog live in. They cry some more. The girls' security guards are thoroughly disoriented and have no idea where they are. They fear the worst for their fellow guard, Andy. From this point on, a guard is in the room with them and another with the children around the clock. The guard is holding a sawed-off 12 gauge, and neither the children nor the security guards think they have any chance of succeeding if they try and rush the guard in the room.

5:33 a.m. Ivory and four other former BK gangsters—his current day homies—come to a large three-story Tudor brick house which catches their interest. Every light in the place is on, and the front door is open.

"Suspicious," says Booker T. Smith, the best watcher and man-hunter in Ivory's retinue.

"Let's find out what's up," Ivory orders, and the car stops abruptly and empties its five occupants.

Five minutes later, the five have given the "clear" notice for every room in the house.

"Lots of food, no people. Steel doors and rooms without windows. An empty pair of cuffs, and rolls of duct tape. This is the kidnappers' safe house. They must have boogied outta here less than ten minutes ago," announces Booker, stating the obvious.

Ivory nods and orders the men back into the car. He taps McGee's phone icon.

"It's me, boss. We found the place, but we're too late. We'll check with the cops. They are already on it; so, we won't be violating our agreement with Damien."

"Okay, but make the call an anonymous one on a throwaway. I don't want Damien to go berserk because we dissed him. I presume they have headed south into the low country. You guys head for the Bronx and Five Points. I'll round up three more sets and have them hit Brooklyn and Spanish Harlem; Caitlin and I will head for Red Hook. Let's touch base every couple of hours."

McGee turns to Angelina, "The cops are involved—nothing to do with any of our activities. A little girl was seen running from a man dressed in black earlier last evening, then very early this morning a girl was manhandled and thrown into a big SUV. That resulted in a preliminary Amber Alert and a heavy duty police search throughout Harlem and now through the city. Ivory and his homies found a house in a nice Upper East Side neighborhood with its doors open and lights on. They went in and found evidence that people had been held prisoner there. There was lots of food, no people. Steel doors and rooms without windows. An empty pair of cuffs, and rolls of duct tape. There was the kind of food kids eat in one of the rooms. We can only presume that this is about your girls. Right now, the police don't have a name for the girl they are looking for. You and Damien are approaching a crossroads about telling the NYPD or the FBI what has happened. Do you want me to call him and get that dialogue going?"

"I don't know what to do. Maybe we'd better talk to Damien. This sounds like it is getting dangerous."

"Not necessarily, Angelina. If all of this is related to your daughters, then it would appear that they are still very much alive and are being protected because they are such a potentially valuable asset."

Before McGee can make the call, Angelina gets another call from the kidnappers.

"Did you call the cops, lady?"

"And hello to you. No, sir, we did not."

"Who's we?"

"My husband and I. We saw the news. Apparently, you lost control of one of our daughters, and several people called 9-1-1. Still we just kept quiet. We have the money ready, and we have done everything you asked so far. Don't hurt the girls. I'm ready to leave for Europe and Turkey as soon as you give me the rest of your instructions. Nothing's changed at our end."

"I'm gonna believe you for now. So, here's what you need to know: go in person to Deutsche Bank Bonn and ask for Herr Derrick von Krankenheiser, who is a senior accounts manager. Show him the documents from your bank or insurance company or whatever which verify that you have the money ready for transfer, and he will set up an account that can work smoothly with the Turkish bank. He knows absolutely nothing about my end of this transaction or that this is related to ransom. It is against German and Turkish law to be party to a ransom transaction; and the whole deal is off; and you won't see your daughters again if Krankenheiser gets suspicious. *Apprendere?*"

"I understand."

"One last thing: get an iPhone and arrange an account that allows use in both Germany and Italy. Call me after each step in the process. I can be reached at these burner phones: 845-308-6682 tomorrow, 845-308-2195, day after tomorrow, 845-308-9362, the day after that. Don't bother trying to trace them. The phones will be discarded after each of those days. You get all that?"

"Yes."

"Then you better get moving; you have a lot of travel arrangements to make in a short time."

The caller hangs up.

Caitlin excitedly says, "Those cell phone numbers are Red Hook area codes. Maybe we're catching a break and are going to be able to narrow the search."

"What're we waiting for?" McGee says. "Let's get on the way. You call Ivory and I'll get hold of the other three sets of searchers; and we'll all head for Red Hook. After the Wednesday's Child case, we are pretty familiar with the territory."

"We are pretty popular with the Catholic community there after our help in bringing all of the St. Anne's orphanage girls back. They'll help us look," Caitlin says.

She turns to her number two, Grant Lathrum, and asks, "How 'bout you getting in touch with Sister Ophelia at St. Anne's and set up a meet? Tell her only that we're trying to find a couple of missing girls, and we need their help in a big way."

"Consider it done, boss," Grant says.

Angelina says, "This sounds promising. I'll call Damien and finalize the arrangements to use his corporate jet. I should be able to leave late this afternoon. I'll keep you posted."

Ivory and his homies are in Five Points in the central lower area of Manhattan when Caitlin calls. They have been

conducting a fruitless search of the many tenement buildings lining the streets in the area and are just passing a block
where the Tombs [officially the City Prison Manhattan] is
located—125 White Street. Ivory is driving. He makes a
completely illegal bootlegger's turn in the middle of the street,
and they head for Red Hook neighborhood in Brooklyn. His
number two, Booker T. Smith—sitting in the shotgun seat—
holds on with both white-knuckled hands.

David Harger and his senior technical assistant, Craig Yankovich,
and Caitlin's assistant, Rosalie Hertel, are trolling through the area
of Spanish Harlem between 96th and 108th Streets—the area that
has thus far missed out on the city's gentrification program, and is
still the "Black Mecca"—with no more success than Ivory and his
car load when Caitlin reaches Rosalie on her cell.

"That was Caitlin," David says. "We're leaving SoHa as fast
as we can do it. Get us to Red Hook!"

The rendezvous point is St. Anne's Orphanage near Red
Hook Houses East, a huge drab dark red brick government
project housing center. Sister Ophelia, abbess of St. Anne's
nunnery and senior sister of the orphanage; Father O'Leary
of the Assumption of Mary parish; and Brigid O'Hanlon,
one of the rescued girls from the Wednesday's Child interna-
tional kidnapping and rescue case—whose intrepid actions
during the grueling period of captivity by Snakehead Gang
human traffickers earns her the right to be part of the search
that David Harger calls the Catholic sisters and Brigid about.

Sister Ophelia takes charge as soon as McGee's people
gather in the orphanage chapel.

"Brigid and I, and Father O'Leary have been on the phones
since you called, David. We are eternally grateful for all that

the McGee people did during the Wednesday's Child case. We have a phone canvass underway already, and in half an hour to forty-five minutes we'll have maybe two hundred people coming to St. Anne's for instruction in how to conduct this search. How long have the girls been missing?"

"Two days," McGee says. "I can't thank you enough for volunteering. You people are able to blend in and not attract attention to yourselves—a lot better than we can. We are grateful to have your boots on the ground."

"We're only too happy to be of whatever help we can," says Father O'Leary.

The "ground" to be covered is largely a multi-ethnic and polyglot crime-ridden slum. The location now occupied by the Red Hook Houses was the site of a shack city for the homeless—called a "Hooverville"—in honor of the despised US president at the time. Red Hook as a whole and the Red Hook Houses especially are ringed by a nearly impenetrable barrier of slums. No child or woman would ever consider stepping out of one of the project buildings in the dark, and police do not come in the night except in the direst of emergencies and then only with a small army of officers to watch each other's backs. The search will—of necessity—have to cover the industrial waterfront, the fetid sewage polluted Gowanus Canal area, and the adjacent Carroll Gardens. Gowanus Canal and its environs which is a cesspool of crime, violence, and drug abuse whose only saving grace is that it provides the principal means of entry into Carroll Gardens. That neighborhood has an element of charm—tree-lined streets, beautiful old brownstones with front and back gardens, a diverse array of restaurants and bars, good local delis and Italian markets. The main charm is that it is away from the Gowanus neighborhood. Carroll Garden's Smith Street is constantly buzzing with inebriated foot traffic with a bar between every other storefront. The search crews do not plan to search there for a long time for the very fact that it is too nice a place.

Caitlin gives the gathered crowd of volunteers pointers on how to look, see, and not be seen.

"Remember, you have an equal value to the girls for whom we are searching. We do not want anything bad to happen to you. Don't linger too long, make too many passes, or otherwise call attention to yourself in those worst areas. If you see something suspicious, call in. If you see something dangerous, take no action yourself. Call us or the police. We are determined that none of us will come to harm during this mission.

"We are looking for two big black SUVs, but the kidnappers have probably ditched them by now. Ride with your windows down; walk slowly and all the time look for something out of place. Is a girl waving at you from an upstairs window? Is there a crude sign calling for help or displaying 'SOS,' or anything else to get your attention? Go with a partner, never alone. If you are approached by thugs or maybe even suspicious kidnappers, run, scream, call 9-1-1, or whatever it takes. Check in to headquarters—that's here at St. Anne's—every hour. Sister Ophelia and Brigid will be manning—or *womaning*—the phones. While I've been talking, McGee, Ivory, David, Craig, and Rosalie have marked up a map of Red Hook into search sections. Sister Ophelia and Brigid will keep a record of what areas have been covered."

Booker says, "Me and the homies will be organizing the vehicles. Our main job will be to patrol around and make sure you don't run into any nice boys who forget their manners and need an attitude adjustment. Think of us as the safety inspectors."

Booker is a very large, very powerful-looking man with a shiny bald head, a single gold earring, and a wifebeater shirt. He works out, and his 250-pound frame is lean for all of its size. He is compact and has two gold front teeth with cutout stars which reveal the underlying brilliantly white incisors. He looks like a pirate about to overrun a crew trying to repel boarders. Ivory is a tall powerful man with very well-defined muscles. He has a lean and hungry look, like Shakespeare's Cassius. He is no less an imposing creature than Booker, and no one has any doubts about the man's ability to preserve and to protect those for whom he is charged to defend. The volunteers are—to a person—all glad to have Booker and Ivory on their side.

Sister Ophelia smiles at her passing memory of Caesar speaking about men he wants and those he fears, *"Yond Cassius has a lean and hungry look He thinks too much; such men are dangerous."*

Chapter Ten

Angelina Paxton/ Desireé Markee flies to Frankfurt in her husband's 2014 Embraer Phenom 300 private jet. She is accompanied on the flight by Earl Hansen and Olivia Zenger, former DSS [US Diplomatic Security Service] special agents who are acting the roles of "valet and personal assistant" in public. The DSS is the federal law enforcement arm of the United States Department of State. Former Special Agents Hansen and Zenger were members of the Foreign Service charged with protecting diplomats before they became well-paid senior officers of McGee & Associates Investigations working under Ivory White. The two officers are not known to people outside the firm, and they are discreet to the point of being tedious about secrets. They will shadow the woman whom they know only as the mother of kidnapped children who is, herself, in danger. They will remain in constant contact with Ivory, and Ivory will update McGee regularly.

Mrs. Paxton exits the plane within five minutes of taxiing to the VIP private hangars of [FRA] *Flughafen Frankfurt am Main* escorted only by a liveried valet and her personal assistant. Ten minutes after that, the kidnappers in Red Hook, New York, are aware of her whereabouts and the route of her travel to Deutsche Bank Investment & FinanzCenter on Friedrich-Breuer-Strasse, Bonn.

The Mercedes drives to the rear VIP entrance of the bank where she is met by Herr Derrick von Krankenheiser and escorted to the fifth floor offices of "Special Investments."

"We are pleased that you have chosen Deutsche Bank for your business, Mrs. Paxton. We were informed that time is of the essence. Would you care for a glass of wine while our transaction is underway?"

"No thank you, Herr von Krankenheiser, but a glass of water would be nice."

The bank officer turns to a secretary and says, "*Wasser für Frau Paxton, bitte.*"

"Now, do you have the bank name and account number where the money is currently being held?"

"I do."

She gives him the information.

"Excuse me, please. I will communicate by e-mail with my counterparts in the US and Istanbul. It will not take long."

"I'm fine."

Twenty minutes later, Herr Krankenheiser returns.

"The funds are presently residing in account AP05/22/2020SPI, TExpress25MUSD. It will be necessary for you to have this number immediately available to complete your transaction in Turkey. At the Finansbank, you will conduct the funds transfer and receive your bearer bonds in TL [Turkish lira] with the help of bank vice president, Bey Erbey Kızılkaya. Finansbank will provide full security for you as long as you are on Turkish soil or in Turkish airspace. I have a printout for you. Have you any questions, Mrs. Paxton?"

"No, sir. Thank you for your service. I need to be on my way. There is a time-sensitive issue in my business needs."

"I wish you a safe and pleasant journey, then."

Angelina leaves the VIP private hangar in Frankfurt one and a half hours later, bound for Istanbul. As promised, Bey Erbey Kızılkaya and a staff of four meets Angelina and her "valet and assistant"—Earl Hansen and Olivia Zenger—who pose convincingly in their benign roles.

It is after hours when they touch down in IST [Istanbul Atatürk Airport], and the three of them are exhausted. They take a taxi to the Sheraton Istanbul Atakoy Hotel and crash for the night. They sleep in and have a big breakfast before calling the bank. Angelina calls Finansbank and the receptionist assures her that a limo will be along presently.

As promised, a limousine arrives at the hotel's front door, and Angelina, Earl, and Olivia are whisked to the Finans Bank Anonim Şirketi on Büyükdere Cad. No: 129 Mecidiyeköy. They are met by the bank vice president.

"How nice to meet you, Mrs. Paxton," Bey Kizilkaya says, offering his hand to Angelina and ignoring the servants.

"I have taken the liberty of having the staff pour glasses of our pleasant nonalcoholic *ayran*, a yogurt, salt, and water mix. I think you will find it refreshing."

Even the servants are given a glass; and, indeed, it is refreshing. It has been a long couple of days.

Because of the size of the transaction and the bank's fee, Bey Kizilkaya and his staff work overtime to produce the bearer bonds. Each bond is in the TL equivalent of $10,000 USD—2,500 certificates, each carrying the notation, "Payable to Bearer." Each certificate is printed on beige-colored 28 pound stock paper the size of a half sheet of standard type paper. After two countings carried out in Angelina's presence, the bonds are boxed into six ream-size packages and sealed in a box with the logo of the Finansbank, Istanbul.

Bey Kizilkaya offers his hand to Angelina and says, "Thank you for bringing your business to us. If we can ever be of service again, please let me know. Here is my card. I am sure that you are well aware of the downsides of bearer bond ownership, but it is my duty to remind you. You will be unable to cash these unregistered bonds in the United States. The applicable law is the Tax Equity and Fiscal Responsibility Act of 1982. These Turkish bonds are backed by the bank and the government of Turkey. The holder of these bearer bonds need only submit certificates to the issuer's agent and can thereby anonymously cash them in for their face value. While that is expeditious and may suit special needs of the bearer, it also creates great risk for you as the legitimate owner. If they're lost or stolen, there is virtually no way to prove who the rightful beneficiary is. In that case, since there is no registration at the time of purchase, the holder—you—who should be entitled to the proceeds—will be out of luck. Do you have any questions for me, Mrs. Paxton?"

"No thank you, Bey Kizilkaya. I understand and accept the risks. Despite the late hour, we need to return to the United States early tomorrow morning."

"Our security service will escort you and the bonds until you are safely aboard your aircraft. I wish you well, madam."

At six the next morning, Angelina, Earl Hansen, and Olivia Zenger are taken in a protective convoy back to the airport from the Sheraton and sink into their comfortable recliner seats on the luxurious Embraer Phenom 300. They still have a sleep debt to pay; so, they sleep almost the entire way back home to New York City.

The search of Red Hook, Brooklyn, is thorough, efficient, well-coordinated, and successfully surreptitious. It takes four days. McGee drops in to meet Dominic Lanza, head of what once was the Colombo crime family in his usual haunt, the Terzaghi Wine and Dine on Hicks. Nothing comes of the meeting; but, nonetheless, McGee is satisfied that the don really does not know anything about the kidnapping of Damien Markee's daughters. That leads to the conclusion that the abductions were not associated with any of the five families either, because Dominic is too well-connected to be naïve about the activities of *la cosa nostra*. The crew takes two days to canvass the stretch of blocks between the Bergen and Carroll train stops. This is Red Hook at its best and raunchiest. The neighborhood offers a dense concentration of bars ranging from historic, to divey, to speakeasy, to sexy cocktail date spots, to rustic wine bars, and to rowdy sports crowds, all with little pretension or attention to updating or maintenance, but with copious character. The result—like McGee's inquiries into the possible involvement of the mafia—is a cipher. The last two days are devoted to an intensive scrutiny—as much as possible without becoming obvious—of the Point and the areas around the projects. Like Harlem, the population is a diverse ethnic, color, language, and religious composition often with dubious citizenship status. Again—like Harlem's lower south end—this section of Red Hook missed out on city gentrification projects.

Most of the area's religious buildings are storefront churches, which operate in an empty store, a basement, or a converted old brownstone townhouse. The congregations have fewer than fifty members each, but there are hundreds of them. The good people of the churches, like all good New Yorkers, respond to questions with an "I don't want to get involved" shoulder shrug. The same responses come from the many cabarets, speakeasies, street artists, and the jazz scene. Street crimes and the murder rate are ten times the average of the more affluent parts of the five boroughs, and it is not surprising that the population is reticent to talk to anyone who is even suggestive of involvement with police.

The project to learn where Cinnamon and Paprika Paxton are being held is not helped by the omnipresence of social ills: Red Hook suffers from one of the highest jobless rates in New York City, teenage pregnancy, AIDS, drug abuse, homelessness, spousal and child abuse, prostitution, and an asthma rate five or six times the national average. It vies with Harlem for the distinction of having the second highest concentration of public housing in the United States. Also, like Harlem, Red Hook has a high concentration of shelters and facilities: homeless shelters, drug and alcohol treatment facilities, and mental health treatment centers. The process of asking questions in those facilities is fruitless and discouraging.

Most of the homes are low-rise residential buildings on avenues or major cross streets. Many have sealed-up residential floors, despite having commercial businesses on the ground floor. All of the McGee and St. Anne's volunteers overcome their fear and repulsion as they talk to the downtrodden inhabitants. Hidden in the alleys and doorsteps of Red Hook—as is the case in the center of many other US cities and in many areas of rural America—is a vast network of invisible, inarticulate, impoverished citizens, and illegal immigrants living out lives of quiet desperation, one paycheck away from disaster. The regular citizens of America—the "citizens"—occasionally see the homeless sleeping in cardboard boxes, panhandling for cash for food or to feed their addictions, or in the news after being accused of a crime, usually a violent one. Most of the American population finds it easy to look the other way. Likewise, the disenfranchised people in much of Red

Hook with their insurmountable barriers of class, income, race, culture, language, education, and life's experience, live by the creed of "Hear no evil, see no evil, speak no evil." They are almost entirely separated from the greater America in which they live. The result is no progress towards finding Cinnamon and Paprika.

Until near the end of the fourth day of effort. Brigid O'Hanlon persuades Sister Ophelia, McGee, and Caitlin to let her have a try. She bravely walks the streets—with an unseen security force of Ivory White's homies shadowing her—amidst the explosion of graffiti on buildings, cars, trucks, buses and school yards. There is trash everywhere. Because of so much shoplifting, grocery stores only operate in very few Red Hook locations, and there are none in the area where Brigid is walking and talking to the down and out. She is a bright girl and knows the desperation faced by the women and their children. More importantly, almost all of them recognize her as the poster child of the Wednesday's Child kidnapping case and instinctively trust the beautiful adolescent.

She stops to talk to a thirty-something-year-old mother of two young girls—both of whom should be in school, but the mother—who was deserted by her boyfriend—cannot afford clothes decent enough for her daughters to be seen in school.

"Hi," Brigid says with her signature fetching smile, "I'm Brigid. Could you take a second to look at these pictures of two little girls who were kidnapped?"

Letting down her guard for a few minutes because Brigid is so obviously not a threat, the young mother says, "Maybe. You're the one that got took from the orphanage by the Snakeheads, ain't you?"

"Yes, and I want to save these two little girls if there is any chance. Have you seen them?"

She looks and then offers, "I might have seen them. I done a little cleaning in a real bad dirty place ... over on Adams Ave. near the Red Hook Houses East."

"That's close to the orphanage where I live."

"Yeah. Anyways, while I was there, I seen a little black girl standing at the top of the stairs lookin' very sad. That ain't all that unusual 'round here, but what was different was that she had real uptown clothes on. Her dress was probly worth more'n all the clothes me and my kids got altogether. It wasn't none of my business; so, I pretty much forgot about it. I got my own problems."

"Think you could take me there?"

"Nah, it's too far. Me and my kids didn't get nuthin' to eat today. We would not be able to make it that far."

"I can get a car to take us. And plenty of food. Please do this for me."

"I'm ascared. If these people are the kidnappers, they are probly killers, too. I gotta think about my own daughters. I just can't do it. I'm sorry."

"They will never know that you or your little girls are involved. See those big guys over there across the street? They are my protectors. Let me call them over, and you'll see. They can keep us safe. It'll take a while, but we can get a car here and get some real tough people to go with you to the building. What do you say?"

"I don't know...."

"What's your name? Mine's Brigid, Brigid O'Hanlon."

"I'm Anna Bella."

"Please, Anna Bella, you are a mother. Think how the mother of those girls feels. She must be half-crazy with worry."

"Okay, but you have to guarantee that nobody can see me. Promise?"

"Cross my heart and hope to die."

Chapter Eleven

Half an hour later, Brigid, Anna Bella, and her two daughters, are sitting at the dinner table in St. Anne's orphanage eating generous helpings of rich chicken noodle soup and soft fresh whole wheat bread smeared with butter and strawberry jam. Sister Ophelia, McGee, Caitlin, Ivory, Booker, Father O'Leary, and seven of Ivory's homies, are gathered around the table waiting patiently until the famished mother and children eat their fill.

Sister Ophelia gives Anna Bella an oversized black hoodie, and Brigid finds her a pair of large opaque sunglasses.

"You sure nobody's gonna see me?" she asks anxiously.

"Absolutely," McGee tells her.

McGee has a reassuring authoritarian presence about him, and Anna Bella relaxes.

They leave the orphanage in three separate nondescript vehicles. The men and Caitlin are armed to the teeth and surround the skinny little mother in a protective human shield which is the equivalent of a scrum by the Chicago Lions Rugby club. She is frightened but feels safe enough to peek out the window as they make the first of three passes by the building Anna Bella remembers.

"Is this the one, Anna Bella?" Ivory asks.

"Yes, sir."

"You sure?"

"Yes, sir. Absolutely."

"Take Anna Bella back to St. Anne's," McGee orders. "Then get back here as fast as you can. We'll surround the place and then move in as unseen and unheard as possible."

Once everyone is in place, Caitlin makes a suggestion, "A woman alone would be less threatening. Let me go up and knock on the door and see if somebody comes to answer. We can get an idea about who—if anybody—is there."

McGee is reluctant; but he knows Caitlin is right; s,o he okays her request.

"Careful. We don't need a hero, especially a dead one. That clear, Caitlin?"

"Crystal."

McGee speaks into his cell phone, "Everybody in place and ready?"

A series of quick "yeses" follow.

Caitlin walks up to the door. She is dressed in an old tee shirt, worn denim pants, and work boots. She is carrying a handful of papers.

She knocks and waits, then knocks again. Then again a third time—much louder. She looks back at McGee's car and shakes her head.

McGee makes the conference cell phone call, "Move in."

The team moves as unobtrusively as possible to the doors and first floor windows as they can, and everyone calls in to announce their readiness.

"Go," McGee says, and a storm of powerful athletic men in black break down the doors and two windows and hurl themselves into the main floor under a screen of flash-bang grenades. McGee's soldiers run room to room and through the smoke and confusion call out, "Clear, clear, clear!" from every room.

Caitlin makes a quick search.

"They were here. There's two suitcases with girl's nice clothes in one of the bedrooms, and boxes of kid type food."

McGee is furious, and his face droops with disappointment.

"We missed them. We were so close. They must have been spooked by Anna Bella seeing one of the girls or by seeing our presumably invisible search teams. I am going to man up and tell Angelina Paxton and Damien the bad news, then I'm going home to get into bed with a fifth of Jack Daniels, assume the fetal position, and turn the electric blanket up to nine."

"We know how you feel, boss," Caitlin and Ivory say, equally disappointed.

Chapter Twelve

Angelina arrives by taxi from the airport to the 142 West 129th Street in uptown Harlem condo late the next afternoon. McGee, Ivory, and Caitlin are waiting in her living room. They each have a key to the condo, and their men have been unobtrusively guarding the place; so, no one can break in or set up a bomb.

She is carrying the boxes of bearer bonds, and the cabbie is carrying her luggage. McGee stands up and gives the cabbie a generous tip while Angelina fetches herself a good stiff drink.

"Do you have the documents?" Ivory asks, leery that—despite all their efforts—there could be a listening device somewhere in the house.

"I do. No problems through customs or in putting the box in the overhead bin for the flight. A nice gentleman helped lift the box into the bin for me. How about you guys? Did you learn anything? Are there any changes in the situation?"

Caitlin tells her, "Angelina, we do have news. We got a tip and found the new place where the kidnappers were keeping the girls. We told you about it during our last communication with you as soon as you got off the plane. Maybe you were too pooped to comprehend after that transatlantic flight. Unfortunately, by the time we could get there, they were already gone. It's almost as if they were tipped off. The only people who had the exact information about that place were the three of us, Sister Ophelia, and Brigid O'Hanlon...oh, and you, of course. Our partnership survives and flourishes because of our absolute loyalty to each other and to our clients. And you are their mother. We are probably just overly suspicious and mad because we lost them. We have launched an all-out search through the day today and turned up nothing."

"It is heartening to get another tidbit of evidence that indicates that they are alive. Look, this news comes as kind of a shock; so, I think I'll go to my room and try and think things through. I'll be out and ready to resume the fight in about half an hour."

"We'll be here. Try and sleep."

Caitlin busies herself on Angelina's laptop and finds nothing new except two icons she cannot figure out how to open. She makes a mental note to ask Angelina the next time they have a chance to talk. About an hour later, Angelina's throwaway cell phone plays its tune. It is sitting on the coffee table. Caitlin picks it up.

"No ID. This is probably the perps. I'll get Angelina."

She hands the burner to Angelina after the third ring.

"Hello," she says with apprehension hanging in her voice.

"People came to the place where we were keeping the kids. What's up with that? Did you sic the cops on us?"

"I did not, and Damien could never bring himself to talk to any cop except one he owns."

"Maybe. I better not find out you're lying."

"I'm not. Why did you call this time?"

"Have the next set of instructions. Did you get the bearer bonds?"

"Yes, I did. They are in a safe place and ready to make the exchange."

"This is the crucial time. You—and nobody else—come to the back entrance of the Super 8 Motel in Albany. 1579 Central Ave, a few blocks north of I-87.

"I've never been to Albany. Can you give me some directions?"

"Are you stallin' me, trying to have the cops get a fix on where I'm callin' from?"

"Certainly not. I just need to be sure where to go; so, I don't screw up."

"Remember, a lie could be fatal. Well, here goes: Interstate 87 is located entirely within New York State. Get on it from the Bronx approach to the Triborough Bridge and drive pretty much northward through the Hudson Valley and the Capital District. Turn east on I-787 and look for exit 2 onto the 5 and turn north onto it. That's Central Avenue. Follow it until you see the sign for the motel. It's a big one."

"Hang on a second, I'm writing all that down."

She repeats the instructions.

"That's right. Come alone. Bring the paper. No GPS trackers. No helicopters. No drones. No nothin' else. If you deviate in the slightest way, we'll know. Be here at exactly noon tomorrow. Got all that?"

"Yes, sir. Don't hurt my girls."

Click.

Angelina turns to look at McGee, Ivory, and Caitlin.

"Did you hear all that?"

"Got it all."

"Did you record it; so, Damien can hear it, not just hear about it?"

"We did. Now we have to get you ready for the meeting."

"What does that mean?"

"We need to get a tracking device on you and your car and some tiny listening devices on you. We have the latest equipment that the FBI uses...."

Angelina interrupts McGee, "No, no, and a thousand times no! None of that stuff. I am going all alone. You are not to follow me, even electronically. Those are my girls, and I am going to do everything that monster wants to get them back. Don't tell me that I can't trust him. I know all about that. It's still my decision."

"Angelina," Caitlin says, "think about it for a sec. If this goes south on you, there's no recourse. They could get away with the untraceable bonds, kill the children, or even kill you or kidnap you. Who knows what people like this are capable of? Just think about it."

"I already have. It is a terrible decision to have to make; but I have to do something; and this is the best thing to do of all the terrible possibilities. Don't get in my way."

Angelina's eyes are burning, daring anyone to stand in her path.

McGee says, "All right, Angelina. It's on you. It is against our advice, and we want you to sign a paper to that effect."

"If it'll get you off my back, I'll sign it. You write one up, and I will take you off the hook."

"Please reconsider, Angelina," Ivory pleads, but he knows it is a lost cause.

She looks him hard in the eyes and enunciates clearly, "NO."

For some reason, Damien cannot be reached immediately. He finally returns McGee's call at nine that night.

"Damien. Come up to Angelina's place. We have something important to talk about, and the phone is not a good idea."

"All right. I have something going at the moment that can't wait. I should be there in about forty-five minutes."

The three partners of McGee & Associates Investigations sit in the comfortable living room chairs to have a short power nap before Damien arrives, knowing that they will need all of their strength to withstand the firestorm that is coming.

Determined not to let Damien dominate her, Angelina takes matters into her own hands. She packs a small bag of the necessaries and slips out of her bedroom window onto the fire escape and as quietly as possible descends to the ground. She intentionally parked her car on the street when she came in for just such an eventuality. She drives away and onto the I-87. She finds a small anonymous, off the highway, Choice Motel in Nyack and hides out for the night.

The three partners are watching TV when Damien walks in. "Tell me," he says.

McGee tells him about the call, the instructions, and Angelina's decision.

"She wants you to hear our recording of the call before you talk to her."

Damien listens to the entirety of the recording with growing dismay and anger. He has nothing to say to the private investigators. He walks directly to Angelina's bedroom door and knocks, although he could just barge right in.

There is no answer to two more attempts, each louder than the first. He tries the knob. Locked. He bangs hard on the door and is once again greeted with silence. He does a spinning back kick and smashes the door off its hinges and onto the bedroom floor.

"Desireé!" he yells as he strides quickly towards the closed bathroom door.

He is in no mood for coquetry or any nonsense about her going to Albany alone.

"Open it!" he yells in a voice that has made strong man incontinent.

He only demands once. When the door remains closed and no sound comes from the bathroom, he kicks it down just like the bedroom door and pushes his way in. McGee, Ivory, and Caitlin are behind him, worried that in his irrational state he could do great harm to his wife.

Damien's face is purple.

"She's gone."

"Where?" asks Ivory.

Caitlin is already looking for how she could have gotten by them. It takes about two seconds to fix her gaze on the window that opens out onto the fire escape.

"She got out through here," she says.

"I'm going after her," Damien says and makes a determined march to the bedroom exit.

"Stop!" say both McGee and Ivory.

He pauses.

McGee says, "Listen up for a minute, Damien. You'll never find her tonight. Her cell phone is gone; so, maybe we can get hold of her."

Caitlin has her on speed dial and gets the terse message, "Leave your number and I'll get back to you."

She shrugs in defeat.

"I am going to that crappy little Motel 8 in Albany right now. I'll get a room and wait around until noon. I'll stop her and keep that meeting from happening."

He begins to leave the room.

"What do you think will happen to your girls—including Desireé—if you do, Damien?"

Damien's face contorts in anger, frustration, helplessness, and sadness. He sags and takes a seat on the couch in the living room.

"It's the right choice for the moment," Ivory reassures his old BK gang leader. "I guess we'll just have to trust her judgment, much as I hate being in that position."

Damien rubs his eyes and shakes his head back and forth.

"You're right. We'd better sleep on it and decide what, if anything, we can do before noon tomorrow."

Damien and the three McGee Associates agree on one thing the next morning, at least. They will drive up to Albany and find a place a few blocks away from the Motel 8. There are differences of opinion about what to do once they are there.

The three men and Caitlin argue and plot, plan, replan, and fight over what to do as they sit around nervously in their Hilton Express Inn room through the morning. None of them is in the mood to eat, and the TV is just a nerve-wracking distraction.

McGee wins the argument for the time being. It is just too dangerous to approach the motel, however careful they might think they can be.

"So, we'll just sit here on our cans until she calls one of us or until we can't stand it anymore, and we call her," says Damien in a rare gesture of defeat.

"How long do you think we should wait before we call?" Caitlin asks.

After a few halfhearted suggestions and countersuggestions, they agree to wait until one o'clock but not a minute longer.

The time moves with glacial celerity. Ten, ten-fifteen, eleven, eleven-thirty... twelve.

"She should be having the meet right now," says Damien. "I like to be an optimist and think that she is handing over the bearer bonds, and the kidnappers are leaving Desireé in the room for a few minutes while they fetch the girls. Happy reunion."

His facial expression does not match his words.

Twelve-fifteen. Twelve-thirty. The four keep one eye on their watches and the other eye looking at the other three people. There is nothing else to pass the time.

One o'clock, straight up.

Damien opens his iPhone and thumbs down to Desireé's number in the phone book. He touches the number. The cell phone rings six times. No answer. He does it again and then again.

"You try, Caitlin. Maybe I'm too nervous to do it right."

She tries, but has no illusions that she will do any better than Damien.

One-fifteen.

"Let's go," Damien says and rises from his seat.

"Okay, but more like a ninja than the cavalry, okay, Damien?" McGee says quietly.

"Of course. I'm not some dumb young kid, McGee."

It takes them twenty minutes to get up close to the motel.

"Angelina's car's not here," Caitlin observes.

"Let's show the manager her picture and watch him every second as we do. He could be in cahoots with the kidnappers, for all we know," says Ivory.

The man shows the four visitors a blank face in response to the photograph.

"Never seen her."

"We're going to check out the rooms. We'll pay for the room of anybody we disturb who doesn't have anything to do with this lady. You are going to come along with us and open every door. There's a C note in it for you if you cooperate," Damien says, and the manager immediately grasps the logic, especially as he locks his eyes with Damien's cosmic blackhole eyes.

The third room they enter contains a terrible shock.

Tacked to the foot board of the bed is a note created from crude cutout magazine letters, "SUCKERS. We got your wife, and we still got your brats. We got your money, too. Want them back? Cough up another 25 mil. Got your cell number from the sweet little mother. Expect a call in three or four hours. Signed: The Smart Kidnappers and two smiley face drawings.

Damien looks as if someone just drove a dull 2 X 4 through his chest. He stands mute, his face contorted in a towering rage which is frightening to the other three—not so much for themselves, but for what erratic actions lie behind that devil's mask.

McGee and his partners scour the room for any kind of a clue, taking care not to touch anything and inadvertently leave their prints.

"I'll get someone from the office to come up and dust the place, but I don't have much faith that we'll turn anything useful up. These places much have hundreds—if not thousands of prints. It'll take months to follow up on all of them," Caitlin says.

Chapter Thirteen

They return to Manhattan and sit in the McGee & Associates Investigations offices waiting for the call with a sense of doom—like the sword of Damocles—hanging over them. The call comes three hours later. It is nine-thirty.

"Hello," Damien says to his cell phone.

"You know who this is."

"Not really. How about a name?"

"That's a great joke, big man. You ought to get your act together and take it on the road."

"So, what's the plan? You seem to hold all the cards."

"How perceptive of you. So, we'll get right to the point. Twenty-five mil in unregistered Turkish bearer bonds by five days from now. Damien goes alone, makes the deposits, makes the arrangements, collects the paper, and gets back to the city in time to field a call at this same time five days down the road. Questions?"

"Proof of life or no deal."

"Oh, slipped my mind. I've been so busy. How's this?"

The kidnapper shows a photograph of all three of his female family members. Desireé is holding the same day's *New York*

Albany Times Union newspaper front page. The cell phone connection is terminated.

"That laughing hyena," growls Damien. "It's one of the greaseballs," he says.

"Take it easy, Damien. Think this through. There's no proof linking this to the mafiosos, but there's lots of pain in store if you think of it as a working hypothesis."

"McGee, I've followed your instructions and all of the crap from the kidnappers. It's time I did something useful. I'll get the truth. Mark my words."

He stands up and marches out the door. The private eyes shake their heads, but presume—correctly—that it is futile to argue with the man at this point. The only hope is that he will simmer down by morning.

Damien is beyond simmering. By the time he reaches his BK headquarters in the East Harlem Men's Club on 133rd Street in Spanish Harlem and sits down in his usual booth, he is at a rolling boil. On the drive down from McGee's office, Damien makes six calls and asks each recipient of the call to meet him in the club. During the next thirty minutes, the men he summons arrive and find seats. Damien gives the club's employees the night off with pay and begins to speak to Phoenix Draper, his insurance agent and trusted employee; Luigi Amara and Modesto Mattaliano his long-time capos; Atticus Whren, the BK enforcer; Alphonso Vergansi, his only Italian underboss; and Hector "Ice-man" Aguilara from Los Angeles. The bodyguards of each of the men—towering and intimidating black men with muscle-builders' bodies—stand behind the men they are sworn to protect at any cost.

"Listen up," he says. "Somebody—probably a goombah—took my wife and kids; no offense to you Luigi, Modesto, and Alphonso. It's just that the operation looks like and smells like a mafia caper all the way through. The main reason I think that is because the guineas have been poking their noses into BK business for the better part of the last ten years. Maybe they think I've gone soft because I got some legit businesses in my portfolio. Whatever, I need you to shake the five families' tree and see what falls out. Alphonso, you take some of the guys and pick up a couple of the big-shot Genoveses. Luigi and Modesto, get your set out on the street and let's see what you can find out about Dominic Lanza and his Colombos and the Bonnanos. Atticus, you and "Dreadful" bring in a couple of Luccheses; and I'll take a coupla the men behind us and Hector and see what we can learn from the Gambinos. Take your pickups out to the Trenton machine mill factory and make them comfortable on those nice chairs with no bottoms. We'll have discussions with them; and, like the cops say, whoever cops a plea first gets the deal. I'm telling you this: we are not leaving that empty old warehouse without answers."

The call comes at midnight just after Damien falls into a deep and dreamless sleep at the end of a very long day. He is alone in his very comfortable king-size bed in Hamilton Heights, and not happy to be disturbed.

"What?" Damien asks.

"This is you-know-who. And you know the drill. We can't keep your brats or your wife much longer. They're safe for now, but either we get our money or they're dead in a month. You do exactly the same thing your unfortunate wife did for the kids. We get the bearer bonds, and you get your family back intact. This is the plan—take notes…."

The voice gives Damien the details of wiring funds to Deutsche Bank Bonn, then to Finansbank Istanbul.

"Call the same cell number your wife did once you get back to the states. Simple."

The caller clicks off before Damien can respond. He is infuriated and curses for half an hour until he was so exhausted that he fell asleep holding his phone. No one—until now—has ever gotten the best of him. Now, he is being robbed, insulted, and made to play the buffoon; and there is nothing he can do about it.

Once he awakens in the morning, he works at being more rational. After all, he reasons, he will still be rich and the insurance will pay out the whole fifty million. He will have his wife and two daughters back, and—with adjustments—life will return to where it had been before the abductions. He will have to institute security measures that would rival Fort Knox, but he can afford it. There is one abiding knowledge that will keep him going. He will never stop his search for the kidnappers, no matter how long it takes. And then....

His men get busy the day Damien gives the orders. They coordinate their strikes, and, by the end of the third day, seven men—one from each mafia family; a representative from the New Conquistadores, the Puerto Rican syndicate that now controls Spanish Harlem; and one from the Hells Angels—are sitting naked in the vacant factory on extremely uncomfortable wicker chairs with the bottoms cut out. Their wrists were bound to the arms of the chairs, and their ankles to the chair legs. None of them has seen their captors or heard a voice. By Damien's strict orders, his men dressed all in black—including gloves and ski masks whenever they are in the echoing room with the prisoners. For three days, they sit there writhing in pain, hunger, and thirst with no explanation as to why they are being so treated.

Then, for two days, each man is subjected to a barrage of questions about who in their criminal organization is responsible for the abductions of Damien "The Kiss" Markee's wife and children. Perhaps most chilling realization for the prisoners is the fact that Damien's name is openly mentioned. They know that they will never be allowed to report back to their bosses. After the weakening and debilitating period of lack of sustenance, they are fed whole wheat mush and skim milk three meals a day to keep them alive and able to talk. Each man is informed over and over that he will be freed only if he is the first one to divulge what "The Kiss" wants to know. They also learn that "The Kiss" himself will be coming soon, and then the questioning will become serious.

Damien takes his corporate jet to Frankfurt and a limousine to Bonn where he meets with Herr Derrick von Krankenheiser in the Deutsche Bank. The transaction is as smooth and simple as a German machine. Like Desireé, he meets with Bey Erbey Kızılkaya at the Finansbank Istanbul and leaves the bank with a box containing twenty-five million dollars' worth of bearer bonds in ten thousand dollar denominations, all in Turkish lira. Unlike Desireé, as soon as the transaction is complete, Damien receives a text message on his iPhone from the insurance company telling him that the company has completed its obligation, and he no longer has insurance. Damien takes two zolpidem sleeping tablets and sleeps like the dead on the plane back to New York so that he can be alert when he goes to New Jersey to complete the work started by his men.

All but one of the men being questioned tell Damien and Hector "Ice-man" Aguilara that their respective bosses are the ones responsible for the kidnapping just to get the torture over with. That only further frustrates Damien. Only Antony De Fiore—Dominic Lanza's man from the Colombo family—resists to the end, refusing to incriminate his boss.

Hector points out to Damien, "Maybe Antony is telling the truth. And maybe, too, the rest are lying to get over the pain."

Damien slaps Hector across the face and calls him "a stupid wetback."

He is no longer able to be rational. He *knows* that one of the crime syndicates is responsible and probably Dominic Lanza.

No one has ever slapped or humiliated the "Ice Man" before and lived. Hector keeps silent.

Damien knows he has made a mistake. But "The Kiss" cannot apologize.

"Look, Hector," he says, "take care of all of these pieces of trash. I give you a hundred K for each, and you can be on your way back to LA."

Hector only nods.

Damien writes a check and leaves him to his work.

Hector knows he is no match for "The Kiss" in a straight up fight. But he has an advantage over the boss of bosses of the Black Knights at this point. He is still rational, calm, and able to act in his own best interests.

As soon as Damien leaves, Hector unties every man, gets him some real food, and brings tubs of water, soap, and a pile of towels; so, they can clean up. They put their clothes back on, bewildered as to what is happening. Hector piles them all into the van and delivers them to Terzaghi Wine and Dine on Hicks Street in Red Hook—the quasi-official headquarters of Don Dominic Lanza, *capo di tutti capo* of the Colombo family.

Hector says to Antony De Fiore, "Take 'em all inside and tell Don Dominic what went on. You don't need to say nothing about me. I'll know if you do."

The weak men limp into the diner, and Hector drives to the nearest bank and cashes his check from Damien before catching a flight to LAX.

Chapter Fourteen

Damien curses a red streak for ten minutes before composing himself sufficiently to make the call.

He dials the burner cell number given him by the kidnappers, and as soon as he hears a response, he says, "I got the bonds. Now what?"

"No nice hello? And I thought we were getting alone so well. Heavy sigh. Well, never mind. Here's what you do: at four o'clock tomorrow morning, you go alone—hear me, *alone*—with the box of bonds and set them in a black suitcase you'll find sitting on a shelf in Herman's Emporium on 108th in SoHa. Know the place?"

"Yeah."

"The suit case in question is the third from the left on the first shelf as you face the wall where all the luggage is displayed. To help you be sure, there will be a small red ribbon tied to the handle of the correct bag. We'll be watching, so no funny business. Your wife and little girls' lives depend on you being a good little boy in all of this."

"Are they going to be waiting for me in the store?"

"Nope. You get them back in a week after we have a chance to prove the bonds are genuine. That requires a trip abroad. You understand, right? Once we have our money, we'll give you a call and tell you where to pick them up. I guarantee that they are all right and have not been harmed. They'll stay that way unless the bonds are forgeries or have that bank robbery powder in the box or some other hinky business. Understand all that, boss of bosses?"

Damien fumes, but he struggles to keep his voice civil, "Yeah," he says and snarls to himself.

At four-fifteen the same afternoon, NYPD Sergeant Detective Mary Margaret MacLeese and Detective First Grade Martin Redworth get the call to investigate a van the units find in a vacant lot in South Harlem. It fits the description of one that the human trafficking unit they head up has been seeking. When they arrive on the scene, they find that it is not their van, but it is of serious interest nonetheless. The rear compartment of the van is covered with blood—copious amounts of blood, some of it not yet coagulated. The blood spatter is so plentiful that it cannot be accurately identified as to arterial or venous or how it got there exactly. The detectives send samples for DNA identification and two days later learn that there is no match in any data bank known to law enforcement.

MacLeese has a hunch.

"Check a sample against blood banks. Go back a year."

That proves to be fruitful, if not entirely definitive. The lab reports finding heavy traces of CPDA-1.

MacLeese calls the head of the lab, "What is CPDA-1?" she asks.

"It's the blood bank anticoagulant-preservative citrate-phosphate-adenine—the newest and best version."

"Can you do a rush job and run the DNA against fairly recent blood bank data bases—starting with about a month ago?"

"That's good detecting, Sergeant. The preservative benefit is only good for about thirty-five days; so, I had my lab rats check back that far."

"And?"

"And, we got a hit. It belongs to one Andy Lusesky."

"You wouldn't happen to have an address or anything else we can go on, would you?"

"We have an address. It's phony, just like the name. Sorry, Mary Margaret, but it looks like a bust."

"I'll do some checking," she says.

For some reason, somewhere in the back of her mind, the name rings a faint bell—more like a tinkle. She puts the name into the missing persons data file. She gets a hit, again more of a partial hit. Andrew Michael Lusesky is connected to a kidnapping that took place about two weeks ago. That information was placed in the data bank only yesterday, which is weird. Another weird thing is that Lusesky does not exist; the name is an obvious fake. That brings the van and its contents to the level of importance. What is important is that the kidnapping involves the daughters of one of the biggest mob leaders in Harlem, Damien Markee, she learns. Mary Margaret decides it is time for some more detecting; so, she and her partner Martin pay a visit to South Harlem.

They learn from an RCI [Registered Confidential Informant] that Markee, the head of the Black Knights, has a sort of old-style quasi-official headquarters in the East Harlem Men's Club on 133rd Street two doors away from a derelict plant on Riverside Drive in Spanish Harlem. The two detectives drive out of 1PP [1 Police Plaza] the next morning and pull up in front of the men's club.

They are met at the entrance by two very large, very black, men, who are obviously packing, probably illegally. The two

NYPD detectives open their cred-packs and show the guards their badges and IDs. One of the security men steps inside for a moment then returns and shows them in.

Damien Markee is sitting at a table surrounded by six large unfriendly African-American men.

"What can I do for you, Detectives?" he asks politely.

"It is more what we can do for you," Sergeant MacLeese says. "We have news for you about the kidnapping of your children, the kidnapping you didn't report."

She gives him a look that is just short of demanding. She lets him have the opportunity to explain. He does not respond.

"What we have is a van full of blood."

That gets Markee's attention, "Whose? My little girls'? My wife's?"

"Is your wife missing, too, sir?"

"All three of them. So, tell me about the blood, please."

Now, the bravado and steely face is gone.

"It is the blood of a man known as Andrew Michael Lusesky. Do you know him?"

Damien answers despite his reluctance to reveal too much, "Not really. I never met the man. But, on the day my daughters were kidnapped, one of their security guards got sick; and Lusesky substituted. He and the other two guards disappeared at the same time."

"There is something a bit off about that blood we found, Mr. Markee. It was not fresh. We found traces of an anti-coagulant used in blood bands mixed in it. We think it is a plant—a phony crime scene—but for the life of us, we don't know why. And have your wife and daughters been returned?"

"Not yet."

"Did you pay a ransom, Sir?"

There is a long pregnant pause.

"Yeah ... twice?"

"How much?"

Another pause. Damien Markee is angry.

"Fifty mil."

"As in millions?"

"You heard me right. I've been had."

That is the most difficult statement Markee has ever made. He fights back tears that are struggling to drizzle down his cheeks.

"I know this is tough, Mr. Markee, but are you expecting them to be delivered to you sometime soon?"

"Supposed to be about a week."

"Okay if we set up a police investigation and give you some help? You'll have to tell us everything you know. It would probably be best to work out of your home, not here."

"I avoided the police because I thought it would keep my family safe. I've been a fool. I know that now. Sure, I'd appreciate the help from law enforcement. I have to tell you that I have been working with McGee & Associates, Investigations. Ever hear of them?"

"We know McGee well. And we respect him. My bet is that he told you not to pay the ransom, right?"

"You got that right, too."

"What's your address? We'll set up as soon as we can get back to 1PP and make the arrangements."

"West 143rd Street between Amsterdam Avenue and Convent Avenue, in Hamilton Heights—the Hamilton Grange neighborhood."

"Nice area. Go home, Mr. Markee. Don't do anything until we get set up. There's still hope; so, don't blow it."

"Yes, ma'am, I'm in your hands."

Damien takes care of business in the men's club before leaving for home. He does not need a detective to tell him all he needs to know. Lusesky's blood was planted in the van. That only became known two days ago according to the detectives. It had to have been an inside job—probably one of his own pet cops. His money, his daughters, his wife are all gone. He is a sucker—fifty million dollars' worth. The only way this makes sense is that Desireé is behind it all. She has been trying to get away from him for more than two years. This was her way out. She was too scared of him to file for divorce; and besides, they have a prenup that says she won't get a dime if she initiates the divorce proceedings. This Lusesky guy—whoever he really is— is in on it. Maybe the other guards as well. Damien does not expect to see Lusesky again, but he knows that Lydia Fairchild and Chet Nichols from the New York Protection Service are bonded, and they will one day be accessible to him. He will get the truth out of them—maybe even get good info about where his money has gone and where his daughters and his treacherous wife are. He will live for that day. No one plays Damien "The Kiss" Markee for a fool.

He drives his Mercedes north towards Hamilton Heights so focused that he is hardly aware of the streets or the traffic. As soon as he turns onto Lexington Avenue, two black SUVs block him at the intersection—one in front and one behind. A man in black showing nothing but his eyes walks up to the driver's side and points a sawed-off shotgun at Damien's head. Damien puts his hands palms up on the driving wheel.

The man in black tries the door, which is locked. He removes a glass cutter hanging from his shoulder and cuts a ten-inch circle of glass from the window. The muzzle of the shotgun stares Damien in the face. He sits frozen. The man with the gun unlocks the door and pulls it open.

"Out," he orders.

Damien is sure this can be worked out. He has been in worse situations before. Most of the time the solution is money; sometimes it is persuasion; and Damien Markee has lots of persuasion behind him in the form of several thousand Black Knights. He is calm. This will pass.

He gets out and leaves his car stopped in the right lane at one of the busiest intersections in the city. The gunman opens the back door to one of the SUVs, and Damien slides in and sits down. The last thing he sees before the hood covers his head is the face of Don Dominic Lanza, *capo di tutti capo* of the Colombos. The man is not smiling. Damien is handcuffed.

"Did you really think you could abduct half a dozen made men from the five families and no one would know about it or get back to you, Damien? For what it's worth, nobody in *la cosa nostra* had anything to do with the kidnapping of your wife and children. You are a fool."

Two days later:

Lydia Fairchild and Chet Nichols step out of a nondescript van on the corner of Adam Clayton Powell Jr. Boulevard and 125th Street. They are dazed from drugs and cannot recall how they got there. Otherwise, they are unharmed. They wonder about their fellow guard from the New York Protection Service, Andy Lusesky; but they do not know a thing about what happened to him. They presume the kidnappers killed him.

Two months later:

Mrs. Delilah Vecchione watches her two daughters—Chiarina, age nine, and Cipriana, age eleven—play with all the free delight that young girls can muster on Marina Grande beach, Isle of Capri. The exclusive resort boasts the biggest beach on the island, adjacent to the harbor hydrofoil dock. The water is always refreshingly clean; it is late morning; and the sun will not leave the beach until mid-afternoon.

It is June 13, and the new little family plans to go into town to join the fun of the Festival of Sant'Antonio, the Anacapri patron saint. They became Delilah—Mrs. Vecchione—Chiarina, Cipriana, and Donatello Vecchione a month ago when they arrived on the exquisite island located in the Tyrrhenian Sea off the Sorrentine Peninsula, on the south side of the Gulf of Naples. The couple's papers are in order; they are obviously affluent. The marriage took place the day after they arrived. It was celebrated in the *Cattedrale di San Gennaro* in Naples. The girls were ecstatic about the grandeur of the cathedral, the ceremony, their beautiful white lace dresses, and all the happy people. They had no difficulty adopting new names; they were used to that.

-THE END-